Praise for Danielle Joseph's *Indigo Blues*

"Fans of John Green's *Paper Towns* (Dutton, 2008) will likely enjoy this quirky novel."
—*School Library Journal*

"Readers will likely be drawn into the scintillating premise and will get a real sense of Adam and Indigo from their alternating narration…"
—*Publishers Weekly*

About the Author

Danielle Joseph was born in Cape Town, South Africa, and now lives in Miami, Florida. She is a lover of contemporary art, indie music, and anything purple. Check out her other YA novels, *Shrinking Violet* and *Indigo Blues*, and visit her online at www.daniellejoseph.com.

DANIELLE JOSEPH

pure red

Woodbury, Minnesota

First Edition
First Printing, 2011

Cover design by Lisa Novak
Cover images: Heart © iStockphoto.com/Perets
　　　　　　Couple Image © Source/PunchStock

Flux, an imprint of Llewellyn Worldwide Ltd.

Library of Congress Cataloging-in-Publication Data
Joseph, Danielle.
　Pure red / Danielle Joseph.—1st ed.
　　p. cm.
　Summary: Rising high school junior Cassia Bernard, daughter of a painter, plans to spend the summer discovering her passion so she has something to put on her college applications, but when her single father starts dating and then agrees to mentor a handsome aspiring artist, Cassia becomes distracted from her goals.
　ISBN 978-0-7387-2743-1
[1. Painting—Fiction. 2. Basketball—Fiction. 3. Dating (Social customs)—Fiction. 4. Mothers and daughters—Fiction. 5. Fathers and daughters—Fiction. 6. Ability—Fiction.] I. Title.
　PZ7.J77922Pu 2011
　[Fic]—dc23

　　　　　　　　　　　　　　　　　　　　2011014156

Flux
Llewellyn Worldwide Ltd.
2143 Wooddale Drive
Woodbury, MN 55125-2989
www.fluxnow.com

Printed in the United States of America

Acknowledgments

I would like to thank the following people and places for inspiring me and helping me bring this book alive.

Delle, *l'amour de ma vie*, the person I can always bounce an idea off of even when he's half asleep. My editor, Brian Farrey, for helping me dig deep into the heart of this story and for shedding a tear. Sandy Sullivan, the master of continuity and logistics. Courtney Colton for all her publicity efforts. My agent, Rosemary Stimola, for being my fairy godmother.

Joyce Sweeney for helping me find Cassia's motive and Adrienne Sylver for reading early drafts of this story. Christina Gonzalez for being my trusty "officemate," and Teri Gotgart Andersen for sharing her ceramics expertise. Linda Bernfeld and the Wednesday Night Critique Group for all their valuable comments. Museum of Fine Arts Boston for having such an amazing collection of art.

And many thanks to Dad, Mom, Cindy, Kenny, Nikki, and Emma, all of whom added color to my childhood; and to my little artists, Marley, Makhi, and Naya, for creating something new every day, even if it's just a mess.

For my mother, who volunteered, year after year, to teach art appreciation at Hunnewell Elementary School.

ordinary brown

Red is the color of passion, but I haven't found mine yet. After my guidance counselor, Ms. Cable, basically told me last winter that I'd be "lucky to work as a grill scraper at Paloma's Diner," I promised myself I'd know exactly what I wanted to do before I turned sixteen. But my birthday was three months ago and I'm still passionless. So that's my goal for this summer. To embrace my heart's true desire, find my reason for living. And by the time I return to school, I'll be so focused that Ms. Cable will go cross-eyed with surprise.

For now, though, I'm sitting here in my living room, completely still. Usually I could rival any store manne-quin, but today I have a crick in my neck and a mosquito bite on my left ankle that itches like hell. If I move, it might break Dad's concentration, and I definitely don't want to start all over again.

I zone out. Try to think of the basketball game taking place later this afternoon. Of the sweat dripping down my back and pooling in my sports bra. Of my new green sneaks skidding across the cement top. I like running up and down the court. It feels good to get my blood pumping. I spent last summer sunning at the beach and watching Dad paint the breathtaking view of the ocean from our condo balcony. That was okay, but it will not get me any closer to discovering my true calling. Nor will it help my "nearly catatonic resume," as Ms. Cable put it. She also went on to say that if I didn't pick up some extracurricular activities and find something I can excel at, I'd just be a blip on the college radar.

I pretended not to care as I huffed out of her office, but truth be told, I don't want to be a blip. I don't need to make a huge splash, but I at least want to make a wave. So before school ended, I asked Coach Heller if he knew of anyplace where I could play basketball during the summer. He said I should give the league at the Y a try. He also told me that it was a great idea, because I handled the ball well in P.E. So I got to thinking, maybe *this* is my thing. Maybe it's something I could be really good at. I've always enjoyed playing basketball with friends, but besides P.E., I've never had any formal instruction.

Thankfully, I got Liz to join with me. She played school ball our freshman year, so she was all for it. We practiced at the hoop in her driveway the entire weekend before our first day. She taught me how to block shots and go up for rebounds so I wouldn't make a dumb-ass of myself. I guess that's what best friends are for.

I can't hold off any longer. I reach down and scratch my ankle. I have to.

"Ay, Cassia, I'm almost done with the highlights. Sit still." Dad dips his brush into the brown oil paint. He says my hair color is hard to recreate. I thought brown was brown. The color of mud, chocolate, and tree bark. He says it evokes energy and relaxes the soul. Maybe if this living room was painted brown instead of fuchsia (joy, compassion, and prosperity), I could take a nap.

Every year, shortly after the last day of school, Dad gets all nostalgic and paints a portrait of me. He says he's celebrating the fact that I'm a year wiser. All I gained this year were a few pimples and size-ten feet. I hope none of that shows up on my portrait. School's been out two weeks, and thank God sophomore year is over and Dad's almost done with my mug shot. Don't get me wrong. My dad, Jacques Bernard, is a great artist, but there's only so much a girl can take. Two more years of school equals two more portraits. Unless he follows me to college.

I straighten up again and sigh. I hope I get a lot of playing time in the game today. At our scrimmage on Tuesday I played two quarters. Not bad for a rookie with no formal training, especially with two Amazons on the team.

I roll my eyes to look at the clock on the wall. Thirty minutes until we have to be in uniform on the court. Coach

Parker already made it abundantly clear that she despises tardiness: "You're late! Take a seat on the bench!"

"Dad, I've got a game in half an hour," I say, keeping my lips as still as possible.

"Perfecto! Your hair is like silk." He tilts his head to the left, then to the right.

My neck is beginning to freeze up. My mouth is Sahara-desert dry. I instinctively lick my lips. "Can I at least get a drink?"

He takes the brush, dips it in a cup of murky water, and runs it back over the painting. I watch his arm move the brush up and down the canvas with delicate strokes. He looks like he's conducting a sleepy orchestra. He steps back a few feet and smiles. His thick black hair sticking up in all directions, coupled with his animated smile, makes him look like an exclamation point. I can't help it. I smile, too.

"How do I look?" I ask.

Dad blows me a kiss. *"Magnifique, ma cherie!"*

"Good." I pull myself out of the papasan chair. My legs are numb and tingly. It takes me a second to steady myself. Dad stands next to me as we soak in the painting. I pull my hand up to my face and run my finger over the bridge of my nose. I never realized how long it was. I graze my cheekbones; are they really that high?

Still, I look so…ordinary. Not like the cover of Cosmo—more like the girl in a phone book ad for sedation dentistry. *Poor girl, she doesn't know what she's getting herself into.*

I close my eyes and quickly open them again. The painting stares back at me. Creepy. Even after all these years, I'm still not used to having my likeness up for all to see.

I take one last glance before running to my room. I trade my teal sundress for a red reversible tank, gray shorts, and Reeboks. My hair is up in a ponytail and I'm back in the living room in less than three minutes.

I walk past Dad. "I'll be home around eight. We're getting pizza after the game."

I swing open the fridge to grab my water bottle. The emptiness inside glows. A stick of butter, two partial heads of lettuce, and a liter of Perrier, all huddled together on the top shelf. I throw the lettuce into the vegetable drawer, tuck the Perrier into the side door, and put the butter in the shelf marked *Dairy*. I glance over at Dad. His eyes haven't moved from my portrait, prickly stubble framing his face. It's almost three p.m., but he's still in his undershirt and plaid boxers.

"Dad, want me to bring you home a couple of slices or an egg salad sandwich?"

He pulls on a tuft of hair but doesn't answer. There's no way he's having butter and lettuce for dinner. Maybe he has a date. Someone willing to take him out for a four-course meal and a stroll along the beach.

I grip the side of the door. My knuckles turn red. Then white. "Or maybe you want to come to the game. And join us for dinner. There'll be other parents there, I'm sure."

His eyes don't leave the painting. "You look so much like your mother," he mumbles, then lights a cigarette.

My eyes go wide. "Really?" He's said we have the same smile or posture before. But he's never actually said I look like her. And even when a relative or old friend comments on the resemblance, he just clams up.

He takes a drag of his cigarette and exhales. I wait for him to speak, but he doesn't say anything more.

I glance at my watch. Fifteen minutes until pre-game warm up. Exactly the time it takes for me to walk to the court. It kills me to be late, but it's not often that Dad mentions her. Mom.

"Did she like having her portrait painted?" I ask.

"Mmm, yes." Dad looks up from the painting.

"But did she like sitting still?" I play with the spout of my water bottle.

Dad's lips part. It looks like he's trying to say something but somebody has muted the sound in the room. Even the air conditioner is quiet. He stubs his cigarette out in the ashtray. "You don't want to miss your first game."

So he *was* listening.

red for victory

I speedwalk the twelve blocks to the basketball court. Despite the heat, near ninety degrees, there are tons of people out today. Most are in bikini tops, sarongs, and flip-flops, heading to and from the beach. Only a few crazy people like me are actually exerting energy.

A group of girls drives past in a BMW convertible, "no you're not dreaming, it's really me gleaming" busting through the speakers. The girls are throwing their heads back to the music and laughing. I think they go to my school, but I can't be sure. Dolphin High is a big place. With over three thousand kids roaming the campus every-day, I stick to my usual group of four—Liz, Skyler, Anna, and me, all friends from Sands Middle. This summer, it's just me and Liz. Anna's at her grandparents' farm in Peru and Skyler got into a math-nerd program at Harvard.

I stop at the crosswalk and wait for the light. The court

is easy to spot from here. It's near the street, but thankfully separated from the traffic by a big chunk of sidewalk and a short walkway, or else we'd be in danger of pegging people with our three-pointers. Behind the court is a grassy area for soccer, and a baseball field. On the other side of the park building are the tennis courts and a little-kid playground, where I used to spend hours on the tire swing and monkey bars.

My teammates are already warming up. I look at my watch—two minutes left. I hit the light again. The walk sign finally comes on and I jog across the street. Maybe if I stretch my way up the sidewalk, Coach Parker will think I was here all along.

I can't wait to find out how Liz's date went last night. I yank the metal gate open and shimmy around the edges of the court to get a place next to Number 3. That's been Liz's lucky number ever since she eyed the Miami Heat's Dwayne Wade. She looks like a coconut sandwiched between two palm trees—Kate and Zoey. But what Liz lacks in height, she makes up for in speed.

Liz has her hands high in the air, stretching from side to side. I take the spot right behind her. Coach looks at her watch and frowns, but doesn't say anything. I now realize when she says be here at three, she really means 2:55. Unlike my dad, who actually means 3:25 because he's notoriously late.

As usual, everything about Coach is precise. Her coffee-colored hair is cropped short and meets evenly on both sides. There's not a wrinkle in her shorts or tee and her laces are tied with perfect symmetry. Dad would not last a minute on her court.

"How was it last night?" I whisper to Liz as we're crouching close to the pavement.

"Amazing." Her long chestnut ponytail swings to the side. That thing could be considered a weapon. "Harry sure knows how to kiss!"

"Sweet! He's hot." We exchange high-fives. Coach Parker barks another order. "Tell me more later," I say. Harry's been after Liz for a while. At first she dismissed him as a dork, but after watching him sweat it out during a lacrosse game, she finally broke down. I'm glad she said yes.

We warm up for another five minutes. Twelve red jerseys stretching back and forth. Red, the color of warmth, excitement, and cheer (and of course passion). The Miami Heat, blood, and cayenne pepper. Also the color I'll end up after this game if I don't slather on some sunblock. I quickly smooth the lotion over my face and shoulders.

"Did I get it all?" I point to my face.

Liz touches the center of her nose. "Just a little here."

I wipe in the cream and follow Liz to the bench. I drop my bag and plop down next to Kate. Suddenly my size-ten feet and oversized hands don't look so huge. I wonder if the men's department is her hookup for shoes and gloves. She's 6'1", the tallest girl on the team, even taller than Coach. I thought I was tall at 5'8" until I met her.

We're all waiting for Coach Parker to finish talking

with one of the program directors. Kate glances over at me. I'm compelled to talk. "Hey, Kate. Should be a good game."

"Yeah." She looks me straight in the eye. "And don't try and steal my thunder. Just because you did well in practice doesn't mean you know how to play."

Wait a minute; are we at the same place? I look around the faded court, up at the rusty pole and weathered backboard. I don't see any sign placing us in the WNBA. No, this is summer league at the YMCA—all can play. Like a few other girls here, Kate also plays for our high school team during the school year. My team experience consists of me and my friends playing a mean game of horse at Skyler or Anna's house.

"*Moi?*" I squeak.

"You heard me, Cassia. I've been playing for four years. I know what I'm doing." Kate stretches her arms out to either side. Her elbow jabs me in the ribs. Is that supposed to intimidate me? Well, it does. How can she think I'm a threat? Like I'm going to go from one summer at the Y to varsity ball at school.

Kate gets up to refill her water bottle and I nudge Liz. "Did you hear what she said to me?"

"No, what?" Liz smacks her gum.

"How could you possibly miss that?"

"Sorry. Teri was showing me her new belly-button ring."

I let out a huge sigh. "She told me not to steal her thunder."

"Loco bitch." Liz rolls her eyes. "I'll get her later."

"No, no, let it go. It's nothing." I don't need Liz getting us kicked off the team.

Coach Parker motions for us to gather in a huddle. I stay clear of Thunder. Somehow I end up next to Coach. Her shoulders are broad and by the way she stands, it seems like she's in position to block a tackle. Maybe she played college football. With a helmet on she could easily be mistaken for a guy. If necessary, she could squash Thunder.

"Heavy on the defense today. The Blue team has some aggressive players. Look out for Numbers 45 and 22." How does she know this stuff? We've only had one scrimmage so far. Maybe they were on her team last year. Or maybe, in her free time, she's a scout.

"We have them covered, Coach," Maria yells, even though we're smushed together like sardines, our heads pressed against each other. Zoey's sweaty hair sticks to my face momentarily before we pull out of the huddle. *Nasty.*

Coach glances at her clipboard and calls out the names of the starting players.

Thunder snickers at me after her name is called and not mine. Gee, what did I do? This girl definitely seems psycho.

I take a seat on the bench next to Liz. Liz's mom and little sister, Crystal, wave from beach chairs on the side of the court. There are a bunch of other parents hanging around, too. Some in chairs, a few in the tiny patch of shade under the big oak tree, and others sprinkled on the two metal benches. I wipe my forehead with the bottom of my shirt. Sweat's dripping down my face and I haven't even begun to play. I chug some water.

The whistle blows and the game starts. Reds and Blues hustle back and forth. Thunder makes the first basket. A couple of guys in baseball hats hoot. What if one of them is her boyfriend? Poor guy!

Maria zooms across the court. She's good at guarding the ball, too. I guess Liz's crash course paid off because I'm following everything that's going on in the game.

Blue team fouls and the ref blows his whistle.

"Eleven, in," I hear someone scream.

"That's you, Cass." Liz gives me a wake-up slap on the back. "Go get 'em!"

"Now?" I stand up.

Coach cups her hands and yells, "Move it!"

I dash onto the court and the whistle blows again. It's Red's ball. Number 45 is right in front of me trying to make a block. She's flailing her arms around like a wild monkey. I do the same. I'm glad nobody I know is watching. Number 45 knocks the ball from Alex, but it bounces off her chest and I snatch it.

"Go eleven," I hear a few people scream. Without even thinking, I dribble toward the hoop. Number 45 is glued to me like an acrylic nail. I look to my left. Maria's only a few feet away. She has her hands up but she's totally blocked by Number 10, a tall blond girl with a ribbon of sweat dripping down her forehead. I look to my right.

Number 6. Short black hair and braces. There has to be someone to pass to, but nobody is open.

I peer up at the net. It seems so high, so far away. I aim and shoot. The ball bounces off the backboard and slides into the net. *Holy crap, a three-pointer!*

Applause erupts from all sides of the court. I arch my back and smile. *What do you think of me now, Ms. Cable?* I think of the mole on her face and her tightly knit eyebrows glaring down at me, about ready to jump off her face and shake me. "Get a hobby, a sport—anything looks better than blank space. Do it now, Cassia, before it's too late." You would think she was talking to a thirty-year-old, not a teenager.

"Nice shot." Alex moves swiftly past me. I look to the side of the court, Coach is smiling. Liz's mom and sister are wide-mouthed too. Sweat stings my eyes. With the back of my hand, I wipe my face and follow the motion to the other end of the court. The white numbers on the backs of our jerseys make us look like paint-by-numbers.

I glance over to the grassy area facing the street to see if maybe Dad decided to show. My stomach churns. What if he's *really* going on a date tonight and that's why he didn't answer me when I asked him to come? If it wasn't for this nameless woman, that's where he'd stand, in the green spot with the perfect view of the game but away from the other parents. Green, the color of broccoli, basil, and St. Patrick's Day cookies. My eyes immediately dart back across the court and focus on Thunder sitting on the bench. Her face is a pale green. Jealousy, greed, and envy.

Where's your team spirit? I want to call out. I shake off the image of her with gritted teeth and fire in her eyes. I shake off the image of my dad with his arm slung around his date and focus my energy on keeping the ball away from Number 45. My arms are spread wide and I guard the ball like a celebrity bodyguard working a rock concert. I manage to grab a few rebounds.

The whistle blows and Coach calls us over to the side for a team huddle. We're up by three, 23 to 20. I made it all the way to the half. I splash water on my face and take a place next to Liz.

"Nice work, Cass." She high-fives me.

"Thanks." I smile. "Lucky shot, I guess."

"You never know, this could be your thing."

"Yeah, right, Liz." I laugh. I guess I'm a rare breed. Most sixteen-year-olds have been playing the same sport for years, but not me. Besides dabbling in drawing and painting, I've never really participated in any extracurricular activities. And now I have to play major catch-up if I ever expect to find my true calling. I was on a soccer team for a few years in elementary school, but it's too long ago to sneak it onto my college applications. I gave it up after Dad pulled me out of school for three months when he was commissioned to paint *Parisian Life* for the American-French Institute in Paris.

While he painted, I wore my box of sixty-four Crayola

Crayons down to the nub. They were my third box since Mom had died. Dad gave me the first box the day after her funeral. Apricot reminded me of Mom because that was the color of her bathrobe. So that was the first crayon to go. Black (at the time I only associated it with death) was the last crayon left standing; well, that and dark yellow-orange, but that was just because it was an ugly color. I haven't worked with crayons in quite a while. Now I mostly like the simplicity of an ebony sketching pencil. What you see is what you get.

———

Thirteen sweaty bodies, including Coach, cling together like Saran Wrap. "Good job out there, team. But don't get comfortable. We're only up by three. Hustle, hustle." She taps several girls on the shoulders. "You, you, you, you, and you are up." Then, as we break free, she looks over at me. "Good job, Cassia."

"Thanks." I smile all the way back to the bench.

I settle down, happy to rest my feet. I watch Liz shimmy up and down the court. She's zips through people almost like they're invisible. She scores a couple of baskets, but Thunder's in the lead with two three-pointers. Hopefully that'll keep her happy for a while.

It's funny to be here at the Y. Dad doesn't play any sports except for the occasional game of tennis, but I wonder about Mom. Did she play ball or run track in high school? She looks fit in all the photo albums. I bet she would've come to watch me play. I picture her sitting under the oak, crossed legged, with the other mothers. She'd be fanning herself with a book, her long black hair tied loosely in a ponytail. Just like the picture Dad painted of her looking out at the ocean on their honeymoon in Mexico.

Thunder's out, Zoey's in. Liz's out. Maggie's in. I'm starting to get the hang of this. The rotation. Play until you look tired. Or until Coach is tired of seeing you run up and down the court without making an impact.

The Blues, calm and cool, are gaining. But an over-saturation of blue is depressing—an overturned sailboat lost in the depths of the sea, a body during the final stages of rigor mortis, Picasso suffering through his blue period.

I'm not going to let them bring me down. They're behind by one point, 36 to 37. I bite my cuticles. Damn, they score another point. Only five minutes left in the game. Alex dribbles the ball to half-court. She's blocked by Number 45. She passes off to Kate. Kate reaches for the ball but loses her footing and kisses the pavement. *Ouch, that must've hurt.* Coach calls a time-out and a couple of assistants help Kate to the bench to assess her condition. Her face has gone from green to translucent. She looks like she's going to hurl.

Coach glances at Zoey, then me. "You, in."

"Me? Okay." I jump up.

I weave my way through the numbers and settle in my position. Center. I'm not used to being in the center. I usually hang out in the wings. I focus my eyes on the ball. So round. So perfect. I wonder how they're made.

A girl from the Blue team bumps into me, nearly knocking me over. I didn't see her coming. "Keep your head in the game, eleven!" Coach yells from the sidelines.

Focus, Cassia, focus. You can't stand still for a second. I move quickly up the court, following the orange circle to its destination. Dribble. Pass. Shoot.

I try to stay open, spreading my arms wide like a bird spreads its wings. Sophia passes the ball to me and I catch it. Thirty seconds on the clock. We're up by one point, 41 to 40. *Don't let the other team get the ball.* I sprint toward the basket. I want to make this final shot. Number 45 moves up beside me. She blocks me like a hat blocks the sun. I can't see the basket. I glance around the court. Alex is open. *Throw the ball to her.* I take a deep breath and Number 45's sweat fills my nostrils. Wish I hadn't done that. I look to the left. Then right. I do the only thing I can think of. The monkey dance. I flail my arms and sway my hips, clutching the ball like a monkey clutches his banana. Then I pass to Alex. Six seconds left on the clock. People are shouting. Alex catches the ball and shoots. She scores!

Red team wins, 43 to 40.

Red stands for victory.

orange energy

It's just after eight when I walk in the door from dinner. Gerry's Pizza has the best slices—I don't even bother with toppings. It's a sin to add anything to their mozzarella. I invited Liz over, but she has plans with Harry, so her mom dropped me off.

Dad is finally dressed. Khaki pants and a navy blue Polo shirt. His hair has been tamed back with gel. He doesn't look like an exclamation point anymore. More like a period. He's at the kitchen counter sipping a Perrier. "Hi Cassia. Where have you been?"

Huh? I'm drenched in sweat, wearing a basketball uniform. Didn't we have this conversation less than five hours ago? "Remember, Dad? My game. Then dinner."

"That's right." He spins the bottle cap around on the counter. "So how was it?"

"We won and I scored a three-pointer."

"Bravo!" He smiles.

"So what about you? Did you go out?" I bite my lip waiting for his response.

"Never left."

Did she come here? I look around the room. The place is a mess. The kitchen floor needs to be mopped, and painting supplies are spread all over the living room. I breathe a sigh of relief.

"So when's the next game?" Dad asks.

I place my water bottle into the dishwasher. Top rack only. "Monday."

"Okay, remind me. I don't think I have anything scheduled for Monday."

"Really?" That would be totally cool, especially if I score a few baskets. "I'm taking a shower."

"We're having a wine-and-cheese thing at the gallery tonight. You want to come? I'll wait for you here."

"Sure. I'll be out in ten."

I like going to the gallery. It's a great place to people-watch. It's easy to tell the artists from the buyers. The artists are people-watchers too, reading the expressions of the buyers, approaching them carefully if an explanation or greeting is needed. The buyers are painting-gazers, soaking in the work, commenting to their companions. You know a piece has generated interest if a buyer doesn't move from it, ignoring the world around them.

My favorite buyer is the crazy lady, Mrs. Murble, who once accused her husband of cheating on her with a painting.

She said that after they hung the picture in their bedroom, he stared at the thing more than her. I don't blame him one bit!

After my shower, I slip on a pair of white capris and a scarlet tank top. I'm sticking with the color of victory for the night. I leave my hair down (it's wavy if I don't brush it) and I join Dad in the kitchen.

"Shall we?" He reaches for my hand and escorts me out the door.

I stumble over a loose spot in the hallway runner, but I grip Dad's hand tighter and don't fall.

"You all right, *ma cherie?*"

"Yes." I smile.

There's a nice breeze outside now and we walk the five blocks to La Reverie Gallery. We've walked this route so many times, I could do it with my eyes closed. Straight past the cafes and clubs, swing a left at the farmer's market, and the gallery's on the corner. Dad's been at the same gallery forever. The owner, Lucien Pierre, is like an uncle to me. We spend a lot of holidays over at his house.

An old weathered guy, with a green mesh tank top and tattered jeans and a paper cup, blocks our path. Dad pulls a bunch of change out of his pocket and drops it into the cup. "Have a good night, Jimbo."

Jimbo shakes the cup and gives us a toothless grin. "Thanks, Jacques. You know, you're the man."

We keep on walking, past the laundromat, several coffee shops, and the Bubble Club. When I was small, I thought the

Bubble Club was a place for kids to blow bubbles. But judging by all the gigantic boobs that go in and out of the place, I now have a very different picture of what goes on inside.

La Reverie sits on the corner of Collins and 57th Avenue. There's Jordana's hair salon on the right and All-Fed Mini Mart across the street—my favorite place to stock up on cheesy magazines that make me glad no one is chasing me, trying to snap a photo of me in a bikini. Now if I had time to glam up, that'd be another story, but it always seems like the celebs are caught picking a wedgie in their sweats or throwing a major tantrum.

From outside the gallery, it looks like they have a good-sized crowd inside. Maybe Dad will sell a painting. Hopefully not *Lady in Red*, one of my favorites. It shows a fair-skinned, bikini-clad tourist sunning on the beach, who obviously forgot to use sunblock. I see this all the time. Don't leave home without your SPF 50.

"Good evening, Jacques. Good evening, Cassia," Monica says, holding the door open for us. What seems like a dozen silver bracelets dangle from her arm. She's Lucien's on-again, off-again, now apparently on-again assistant.

She gives Dad a kiss on the cheek, then me. I walk through the gallery, imagining I'm some super singing sensation just flown in from London on my private jet. Wave. Greet. Smile. Kiss. Exhausted when I make it to my final destination; in my case, the wooden chair behind Lucien's desk. Dad only makes it halfway across the room. He's stuck talking to Mrs. Murble. She has on a long flowered skirt that sweeps the floor and her hair is piled high like a sno-cone. Hopefully someone will catch his distress signal (tugging on his left earlobe) and rescue him. Not me. I like to witness her insanity from afar.

I look up. *Lady in Red*. Still here, in her yellow-wood frame. Not my first choice in frames—it doesn't do justice to the beauty of the painting. It's like a really hot guy wearing suspenders and a bow tie. I'd never tell my dad this, though.

I can't exactly explain the feeling, but the first time I saw *Lady in Red*, I couldn't keep my eyes off of her. She looks like a movie star in her cherry-red bikini and over-sized sunglasses, relaxing on her pale blue beach chair. She's surrounded by powder-white sand, and at her feet sits the ocean. But it's more than that. Everything in the painting is in perfect proportion. It's one of Dad's finest pieces. Next to it is Lucien's *Masquerade*, two couples seated on jumbo-sized wicker couches overlooking a gigantic swimming pool. If you look closely into the clear, aquamarine water, you see a crushed rose at the bottom. Lucien never talks about his love life.

A waiter approaches with a platter of cheese. He hands me a napkin and I spear a few squares with a toothpick. I leave the fancy crackers for the guests because I know Lucien keeps a box of Saltines in his desk. There's an open packet sitting in the drawer; I turn it upside down and watch as the four remaining crackers slide out, along with a multitude of crumbs. I lay two down, top them with cheese, then add another cracker.

I munch on the little snacks and soak in the crowd. Much more interesting than the families at the basketball game. Dad's talking to some lady with short blond hair. She's very pretty. She keeps on grazing his arm and smiling. I wonder if she's the one he's dating.

I feel a strong grip on my shoulder. "I see you found my secret stash," Lucien says. He laughs and crumples up the empty packet.

"Yup. Every time." I laugh too, but my gaze doesn't move from the lioness pawing my dad.

"How's basketball going?" he asks.

"Good." I nod. "B-ball might just be my thing."

Lucien stares at me and strokes his chin. "I can hear the WNBA announcer now: 'Cassia Bernard scores another three-pointer!'"

"Lucien, Lucien," Monica yells, mid-crowd.

"See you later, kiddo." He pats me on the back and rushes over to speak to a man with a really wide straw hat.

I wonder if he was serious. Nah.

My focus is quickly back on the blond lady until she moves on to talk to someone else, giving my eyes a rest. Why hasn't Dad introduced us? How long have they known each other?

I take a small piece of note paper, fashion it into a mini broom, and sweep the crumbs on the desk into a pile. I'm about to throw them away when I realize the garbage can has been moved.

There's one near the door and another in front of a

painting of a homeless woman searching through the trash for newspaper. How fitting.

The garbage can near the door looks like my safest bet; no need to upset the homeless lady. I clutch the crumbs in my hand and weave through the crowd. I avoid eye contact with Mrs. Murble and nod at Dad's accountant, Hank. Somebody is staring at *Lady in Red*. Somebody new. Somebody with a very cute butt! I feel compelled to catch a glimpse of the butt's owner, so I inch closer. Then closer.

We're almost standing side by side now. Without turning my head, I check out the rest of the goods. He has spiky blond hair and is wearing cargo pants and an orange (energy, power, and strength) Ron Jon T-shirt. Orange, the color of basketballs, Mars, and jack-o'-lanterns, cannot survive without red. He looks about my age. I hope. And he's tall, too, over six feet. Bonus! Kids never come here alone, though. With my luck, he's the son of Mrs. Murble.

He's not moving. I wonder if he's interested in the painting in general or just the lady in the bikini. But who am I to talk? I'm staring at his butt.

"What do you think of this painting?" Cute Butt asks. He speaks! Sexy voice, too.

I can't praise Dad's work. Isn't that bragging? I return the question. "What do you think?"

He cocks his head to the side like he's thinking. Really thinking. "I love the realism and use of shading. They bring out the lady's emotions."

Interesting viewpoint. I would've commented on Dad's brilliant use of colors; all the reviewers usually do.

"Yeah, this is my favorite of Dad's paintings." Oops, did I say that aloud?

"Jacques Bernard is your dad?" Cute Butt's emerald-green eyes double in size. He stares at me with the same amount of intensity that he stared at the painting. I feel the heat rise to my face like a 100-watt light bulb overpowering a small room. If you look closely, the lamp has a caution sticker on the top of the base—*Bulb not to exceed 60 watts*. I hope I don't explode.

"Um, yeah." I back up a bit.

"Graham Hadley. Nice to me you." He holds out his hand. Phew, he didn't say Murble.

I extend my hand, uncurl my fingers, and watch as a handful of crumbs fall to the ground like confetti. Most of them land on Graham's black-and-white-checked Vans.

"Happy Birthday?" I laugh, nervously.

Graham grins. "Are those cracker crumbs?"

"Yup." I squat down to try and scoop up as much as I can.

"Working on some kind of multimedia project?" he asks.

He can't be serious. But he kneels down to help me save the poor old crumbs. He's collecting the few that still cling to his shoes. I look at his face. It's unchanged. He *is* serious. Oh, now I feel bad.

"Not exactly." I bite my lip.

"Oh, it's more secretive than that." He winks.

"Right. I'm Cassia, by the way." We both stand up and I hold out my hand. Graham combines his crumbs with mine. I really don't know what to do with them, so I shove them into my pocket.

"Cassia. Cool name. So original."

"Thanks."

"Do you go to Dolphin High? I think I've seen you before," Graham says.

He's seen little old me before? "Yeah. I'm going to be a junior."

"Me too."

I can't believe I've never noticed a guy this cute at school, one who actually knows a thing or two about art. Sure, my school social events are limited, but I'm still surprised that I haven't even gawked at him before.

"Thanks for you help," I say.

Graham arches his back. He's broad and muscular, making my knees quiver. "My pleasure, Lady in Red."

Me in my red tank top and now flushed-red face? Or the painting?

I cannot move. I cannot speak. I reach out my hand to grab a chair, anything for support, but there's nothing there so I clutch the air that stands between us.

"Can you introduce me to your dad?" Graham asks.

Figures. I finally meet a hot guy, and he wants to meet my dad.

fertile green

I walk Graham over to Dad. He stands there, mouth hanging open, like Dad's a superhero. We're talking about the guy who sticks his finger in the tub of hummus and sings sappy French love songs in the shower. But Graham shakes Dad's hand, stares at him, and tells him how he's always admired his work. So while I was watching *Scooby Doo* and playing with my Polly Pockets, Graham was soaking in Dad's paintings at various Miami hot spots.

Dad stops the waiter and grabs a cube of cheddar off the tray. "Is this your first time visiting the gallery?"

"I've been here a couple of times before with my aunt. But I've seen your *La Fleur* collection at the SOBE museum a million times," Graham says, eyes bugged out like he's hoping he got the pop-quiz answer right.

I'm standing next to them, smushing the cracker crumbs

inside my pocket into pixie dust. My face is hooked on Graham's, which is hooked on Dad's.

"A museum regular. That's great." Dad's eyes don't leave Graham's face. Everyone is a potential subject. He studies each feature carefully, even though he doesn't paint people he knows—except lucky me!

A woman bellows over the crowd, "Bye, Jacques." I turn toward the door.

It's her. The blond lady.

Dad just smiles and gives her a fluttery wave. He is *so* dating her. Excuse me while I go puke. I squint my eyes and curl my upper lip in her direction, but she's already flickered away. I'll catch her next time.

Graham and Dad launch into a discussion about mixing colors, Dad doing most of the talking and Graham the nodding. I, on the other hand, am trying to get the blond lady out of my head and focus all my brain power on Graham.

"When I was younger I used to be careless with the tubes of paints." Dad runs his fingers through his hair and knocks a gelled clump loose from the rest of the bunch.

"That's totally me," Graham says, laughing. "But I'm learning to be more conservative."

"I used to be like that with food," I say, biting the inside of my lip. "Order way too much, eyes bigger than my stomach."

Nobody says anything. The celebrity and the fanatic both stare at me with sympathy in their eyes.

Dad snatches a glass of red wine off another tray and Graham shifts his weight back and forth. Then they smile at each other in some sort of secret artist code. I take a deep breath to calm my inner stupidity. *Breathe in. Breathe out.*

"Thirsty." I point to myself and swiftly move toward the mini-fridge in the back. Anything to get away from all that starry-eyed, *oh, how I've always worshiped you* stuff. So here I am, standing in the corner after I've chugged almost the whole bottle of Aquafina, wondering why the hell I'm pissed off. I should be happy that this really hot guy is gaga over my dad. That makes my dad young, hip, and cool. Except what about me? Did they even notice that I walked away? Okay, so you don't have to get an A in psychology (I did get an A, though) to realize that I'm more pissed about the lady pawing Dad than I am about Graham. But why does my dad need a girlfriend now? We were managing fine without her. When he said he was going to try dating again, I thought it meant catching an occasional movie or grabbing a bite to eat now and then. More like finding hang-out buddies, not one specific, potentially desperate woman.

I try to calm down, like I didn't just have a major internal hissy fit, and shake loose all my negative energy. Then I screw the cap back on the water bottle, walk over to the recycle bin, and shoot. Score! A three-pointer.

Dad and Graham are now in front of *Moonlight Bisque*, talking about technique. Dad spent forever trying to get the moon right in that picture. While he was mixing the creamy-colored paint, my stomach had growled, and I told him it looked like the soup Lucien serves every Christmas. Not even ten minutes later, while I was watching *Gilmore Girls* reruns, he yelled out, "You're right! That's it! Moon Bisque"—which later became *Moonlight Bisque*.

"Hey, Cassie." I feel a jab in my side.

"Hi, Thomas," I say, even before confirming it's him. No matter how many times I correct this kid, he still calls me Cassie.

"What's up?" he asks.

"Not much. Just taking in the beauty." I point to the abstract with no name in front of me, but my eyes quickly flit over to Graham to make sure he's still talking to Dad and hasn't left yet.

"Nice." Thomas runs his hand over his shaved head. "Well, I've looked around. Wanna grab something to eat?"

As nice as Monica's nephew is, he's pretty clueless. I'm not sure why he comes to the gallery shows in the first place.

"Sorry, I promised my Dad I would stay and I haven't even made it around the room yet."

"It's good stuff, but how long can you stare at a painting?" Thomas swipes a clump of cheese squares off a tray as the waiter goes by. "I'm starving." He confirms my suspicions—he comes here for the food.

"Well, I have to get back to Dad." And Graham. Geez, I wonder if they know each other. Doubt it, though. Thomas is a year ahead of us in school and plays baseball. He's one of the star players, too. I went with Lucien and

Monica to a game last year, and ever since then he's been really friendly to me.

"Okay, I'll probably head out. Some guys are hanging at the Bristol." He downs the rest of the cheese.

"Cool. Catch you later." I start to walk away.

Thomas is in mid-chew and thankfully does not open his mouth to answer. He nods and throws me a wave. He's not a bad-looking guy or anything, but we have nothing to talk about. I think Monica knows this, so thankfully she doesn't push him on me.

I walk back over to Dad. He reaches for me and gives my arm a squeeze. "Here you are, my love."

"Had to get some water." I move closer to him.

Dad puts his arm around my shoulder. "Graham was telling me he goes to school with you."

"Yeah, we just figured that out."

"But I only transferred to Dolphin last fall. Went to Palm Pointe before that," Graham says.

That makes a little more sense, Your Cuteness, because it means I've had one less year to run into you.

Monica taps Dad on the shoulder. "Sorry to interrupt, but the man in the straw hat has a question about your flower exhibit."

Dad holds out his hand. "Good to meet you, Graham. You'll have to excuse me for a moment."

Ah, alone again. Well, not really alone, but as alone as you can be in a room of more than thirty people chattering about the beauty of art.

I look at Graham. At his yummy, full lips and gorgeous green eyes. And I'm not talking green like Thunder's envy; I'm talking green like life, nature, and fertility. Fertility, oh yeah, now we're talking, baby!

I think he senses me staring at him and smiles. My insides get all fuzzy. I hope that smile is for me, Cassia, not Cassia, daughter of Jacques the Great.

"Thanks for introducing me to your pops." Graham slides his hands into his pockets. "I've been following his work since I did a book report on local artists in the fourth grade. He's a big inspiration to me."

Okay, so the smile wasn't for me, but it still gives me a warm feeling for Dad. To think that some guy my age is sitting home drooling over my dad's art work. I know it's kind of quirky, but I'm proud of him.

"What kind of stuff do you paint?" I ask Graham.

"I started out doing goofy kid stuff like dragons and dinosaurs, but now I'm more into people and places. And abstracts, too."

"Cool. Are you in the art magnet at school?" I notice he has a two-inch scar on his left arm. It's not a clean scar, because part of it is bubbly. I wonder how he got it. Dragon slaying? Scaling Mt. Everest? Bear wrestling?

"Yeah. Just finished advanced painting with Mrs. Sweeney. She's a really cool teacher. What about you?"

"I draw mostly, but I'm not in the magnet. I didn't take any art classes this year. I'm thinking about changing my fall schedule, though; maybe I'll add ceramics or photo. I'll see."

"If you take photo, stay away from Mr. Kim. I think he downs too many chemicals."

I'm not sure about photo anyway. I don't love the idea of going around town snapping people's pics. Pottery might be more my thing. There's something intriguing about molding the clay into a product that you can actually use. "Maybe ceramics then."

Graham pulls his hands out of his pocket and grazes the scar on his arm. Does he know I was staring at it? Am still staring at it?

"Well, you have a built-in art teacher. Actually better than a teacher." He smiles big. Not a tooth out of line.

I shrug. "I guess."

"Sorry, I'm probably boring you. You must hear this stuff all the time."

"No, it's fine." I couldn't ask for better boy candy. Cute butt. Chiseled features. Those fertile eyes again. Who's to complain? "You can come over my place sometime. To see my dad's home studio if you want."

Wait, what am I thinking? If I'm serious about finding my passion, Graham is a total distraction. I need to keep my focus.

He stretches his arms wide. "Really? Your dad wouldn't mind?"

"No, not at all." If it were up to me, the first stop on the tour would be my bedroom. Got a double bed, you know.

Grin. Okay, so who am I kidding? But I can't say no to the owner of such a cute butt.

"That's awesome. You're so sweet." Graham gives me a quick kiss on the cheek. This is so wrong. A hot tamale is giving me a kiss because he gets to see my dad's digs. I don't care; I'm living this up anyway.

"It's totally fine." I walk over to the desk and scribble my phone number on a piece of paper. "Call me."

"Cool," Graham says, nice and slow, like he's trying not to freak out but his insides are shouting for joy. I guess I'd feel the same way if I was invited into the humble abode of, say, an underwear model or blockbuster movie star. But my dad, puhleese!

As we make our way to the door, Graham stops in front of *Uncharted Waters,* a tiny fishing boat navigating the ocean. "What a view!" He breathes in. "I feel like I can smell the fresh salt air."

Our condo balcony boasts this same amazing view of the ocean. It's by far the best thing about our place. Dad's painted our view many times, and every time it looks different. Blue-black skies and water when a hurricane is threatening or pale blues and greens when it's bright and sunny outside.

Being out there on the balcony is one of my clearest memories of Mom. It was just a few months before my sixth birthday. I was so excited about having a Little Mermaid cake, and Mom was outside on the balcony in her apricot Chinese bathrobe. Some days it seemed like she spent all day staring at the ocean, breathing in the salty sea air. She'd be out there when I left for kindergarten, and when I got back she was still leaning on the railing, her black, black hair blowing loose in the wind. She'd call for me to come join her after she heard the front door shut. One day I asked her why she always stood in the same spot. "The sound of the ocean soothes me," she said. I didn't know exactly what she meant by that, nor did I know she was dying. That she had a tiny hole in her heart. That even with all the medical tests she went through, it went undetected. It was a stroke that finally killed her. She was only twenty-nine.

It was an unusually cold day for Miami, so she drew me close and said, "The ocean allows you to see whatever you want to see." I looked up at the swollen black clouds and said, "I see a storm coming." That was the last time we stood there together.

———

As soon as I get home, I dial Liz's cell. *Please, pick up, please, pick up.* She answers on the third ring. "Hey, Cass, what's up?"

I'm sitting on my bedroom floor, against the wall between my bed and my desk. I'm propped up against two huge cushions that used to belong to our old burnt-orange couch.

It's a strong contrast to the rest of the décor. My room is decorated in pink coral and littered with floral designs— white curtains with lilies, four silver frames of Dad's daisy series above my desk, and even a sunflower-shaped waste-basket. You could say I was definitely going through a phase, but Dad was the one who actually surprised me with a total room makeover for my tenth birthday. Instead of updating it, I've just added more things to the room. Most recently, I salvaged the couch pillows on their way to the dumpster. And now that I've met a hot guy wearing an orange shirt, I'm never going to throw them out.

"You bought the yearbook, right?" I ask Liz.

"Yeah, why?"

"Look up Graham Hadley. He's in our class."

I hear her walking, then opening doors, shifting boxes. She had her bedroom painted last week, so she still has a lot of stuff to put away. "Are you going to tell me what this is about?" Liz asks.

I pull my knees close to my chest. "I met him at the gallery tonight. He's really yummy." I hear a shuffle, shuffle, bam, bam on the other line. "Liz, you okay?"

"Yeah. I knocked down a couple of boxes. Yay, found it," she says.

"See him?"

"Still checking." I hear her flipping through the pages. Then she cracks up.

"What's so funny?"

"He has really thick glasses and greasy hair that goes past his shoulders. With some kind of wart thing growing on his nose."

I meet the guy of my dreams and he's really a frog in disguise?

"No way! You must be looking at the wrong guy."

"No, it's him."

What am I getting myself into? He probably went on one of those makeover shows. No wonder I've never noticed him before. "Maybe I need glasses."

"Or maybe you should look up gullible in the dictionary!" Liz laughs, or more like snorts.

"Bitch." I stand up. "That joke is so second grade."

"Yeah, and who fell for it?" She laugh/snorts even more.

"Fine, I surrender. What does he really look like in his pic?"

"Nothing. He's in the back with all the other not-pictured names."

"Only makes him more mysterious." I kick off my sandals and send them flying across the room. "I gave him my number."

"Way to go, girl! You've advanced to the next level of my crash course on how to get a guy." Liz is always telling me to be more assertive. That it's okay for girls to make the first move.

"This could be a real hazard. I'm trying to stay focused on my summer goal."

"The passion thing?"

"Yeah."

"Don't be so hard on yourself. You're playing ball, remember?"

"Yeah, but I should do more. You weren't there in Ms. Cable's moldy office with stacks of student folders that were better than yours stacked up high on her desk. She basically set her hand on top of the pile and told me I was on the road to nowhere." I pick up a pencil from under my desk and draw lightly on the wood.

"Aw, she's a nut," Liz chuckles. "Why should you listen to her?"

"Because she's my guidance counselor. And because I don't want to be stuck at home for the rest of my life. I'm supposed to explore my options." I can't get Graham's green eyes out of my head.

"Suit yourself."

I sigh. "Fine. Do I want to know what the next step of your crash course is?"

"Ask him out."

I left out the part about Graham being the president of my dad's fan club. I can always tell her later, but for now I'll pretend he's mine.

purple power

All day I'm excited about going to practice. We played an impressive game yesterday, so I'm sure everyone will be in a good mood. I didn't get out of bed until eleven this morning because we got home at midnight from the gallery and I had trouble sleeping on account of my slam dunk day—first, scoring a basket in our victory over the Blue team, and then meeting Graham and slipping him my phone number. Double points for that!

I know we only just met, but I have a feeling about these things. For instance, when I met Liz the first day of sixth grade, I instantly knew she was cool. We were seated next to each other in Mrs. Patterson's geography class and Mrs. Patterson wanted to show us the map of the United States but couldn't get the screen to pull down for the overhead. Liz leaned over and whispered to me, "She should show it on her booty, it's big enough!" I almost turned blue holding in my laughter. I know it's really mean, but it was so funny and one hundred percent true. Anyway, we've been best friends ever since.

I make sure I leave home with plenty of time to spare. I don't want to be late for practice. As I reach 64th Avenue and Collins, I hit the surf shop. The window is filled with Ron Jon stuff. I wonder if Graham shops here. Does he even surf? I hope so. I don't need a vivid imagination to picture his hot bod riding the waves. He totally has the surfer look going, with the bleached tips and spiky do and Hawaiian Tropic suntan.

"You're going to be late if you don't stop drooling at the guy inside," a creepy but familiar voice says.

"Huh?" I turn around and see Thunder behind me, Zoey next to her.

I look back at the store to see who she's talking about. There's some short guy in baggy jeans and a wife-beater checking out bathing suits. "Him? Oh, no, I was…"

"Sure," she snickers, then keeps on walking.

The Amazons are a few feet ahead of me and they're giggling. I know they're talking about me. That's plain rude. "Hey, guys, wait up." I pound the pavement to catch up.

Why did I say that? I must be a sucker for punishment.

They don't answer, but they do slow down enough so that I'm next to Zoey. Except it's hard to have three in a row on the sidewalk, so I'm immediately bumped back when we have to maneuver around a bike chained to a parking meter. I end up walking behind the duo for the next eight blocks. They don't say much to me, which I guess is better than insulting me.

When we get to the court, I sprint ahead of them and wave to Ms. Parker. As I'm opening the gate, I hear Thunder growl, "Show-off."

What's it to her if I want to be on time? Liz isn't here yet, so I stand next to Maria. Coach says we're going to stretch for a few minutes, then run some laps around the baseball field. A few girls groan and Coach says if she hears that again, we'll run laps the whole time. Sophia mutters under her breath, "But this is summer league."

Why don't you tell that to Thunder?

Liz shows up as we're getting ready to run laps. "Betancourt, you're late!" Coach yells at her.

"Sorry, there was an accident on the MacArthur Causeway, and—" Liz is still trying to catch her breath.

"An extra lap," Coach says, then she blows her whistle and we're off. Liz rolls her eyes, but luckily Coach doesn't see.

I'm not too good at this running-a-distance thing. The first week I didn't pace myself and was out of breath pretty quickly. Slightly wiser this time, I try to keep an even tempo. I look out at the open sky, not a cloud in sight. It's too hot to stare for long, so I focus my eyes on the leafy trees. Every time I pass one, I relish the second spent in the shade. It's the feeling you get when you can never have enough of something. Chocolate. Cute Butt's rear. A day at the beach with Dad collecting shells. More time with Mom.

I keep to the edges of the field, even though it makes my laps slightly longer. Liz is ahead; she's always been a fast runner. She was recruited for the track team freshman year.

I'm a few feet behind Maria and Kate. I watch their ponytails swing back and forth. They look like witch brooms. Good witch. Bad witch. They both have thick brown hair, although Kate's has a lot of auburn to it. I peer over at the baseball diamond, where a bunch of kids have just arrived for a game. They look snazzy in their little uniforms all tucked in. They're probably first or second graders. This one short, chunky kid is standing there staring at us as we run by. He's so cute.

Coach blows her whistle, thank God. This is our third lap, the last. Everyone runs for their water bottles, except for Liz who's already on her extra lap. After we chug some water and catch our breath, Coach tosses out the balls and we start with lay-ups. I always love watching the basketball players on TV doing lay-ups; they make it look so easy. I grab a ball and hold it in my hand. Coach is working on form today, so she's spending time with each person, perfecting their shot. She instructed us to really get to *know* the ball.

I look down at mine, full of air. The tiny bumps that make up the surface are smoothed over a bit. I move my hand over the top in a circular motion while I wait for my turn. My hands feel numb and sweaty from the rubber.

Tracing the tiny bumps, I imagine what it might be like to read braille. I close my eyes and run my fingers over them until I hit a groove.

"Wake up, Cashew," Thunder barks from behind me.

Oh, aren't we original. I run up to the middle of the court and shoot. The ball bounces off the backboard and rolls to the side. Coach grabs it and tosses it back to me. "You have to feel the ball."

"But I was," I say. I really was. I felt the bumps, the grooves, the smooth parts, the rough parts, and the part where the Spalding name is partially rubbed off.

Coach grabs another ball from the side and cradles it in her left palm. Then she slides her right hand over the top. She instructs me to do the same with my ball. I rub my hand back and forth over the top like an old lady at the supermarket inspecting cantaloupes, feeling every inch of the fruit. Then Coach says, "Now let go, and feel what it's like to release the ball."

I do. The ball hits the dull metal pole, nowhere near the basket.

"That's good." She collects my rebound and tosses it back to me. "Now try it again."

Feeling movement is something new to me. I only think about feelings in relation to paintings, books, or movies. I shoot another basket but miss.

"Take your time until you get the hang of it," Coach says.

I stare at the ball. At the faded orange. It's not like the

orange from Graham's shirt. This orange is the kind Graham's shirt will be after it's gone through the wash a thousand times. I think of Graham and his perfect body. Perfect face. I aim the ball and shoot. The basket is mine.

"That's it." Coach smiles and waves up the next person.

"Make love to the ball," Thunder cackles as I head back to the end of the line.

I want to yell, *That's probably the most lovin' you'll ever get,* but right now that goes for me, too, so I keep my mouth shut.

For the rest of practice, I really try to *feel* the ball. To get to know it. Too bad we can't use the same ball every time. I name mine Baldwin (on account of its apparent baldness and ability to help us win) and feel like we have a special bond now.

At four, Coach blows her whistle and tells us to grab our water bottles and have a seat on the bench. That's fine with me because my Secret clear roll-on for women is just about worn out, and Baldwin needs some air.

"I like what I saw out there today. Good structure and form. If you have a net at home or live near one, try to practice over the weekend. Monday's game is going to be close. Don't underestimate the underdogs." Coach says this like she spilled the winning secret.

After she tells us we're playing the Brown team, it all makes sense. Brown is definitely a camouflage color. They can sneak around us unnoticed if we're not careful. However, too much brown bores the soul. And Ms. Cable made it abundantly clear that it's not a good idea to ride under the radar. "Cassia, for every million nobodies applying to college each year, there are only a few thousand somebodies. Which do you want to be?" She didn't give me a chance to answer because at that very moment she got a call from the principal's secretary alerting her that there was drama in the second-floor girls' bathroom. She cut our session short with a "Let's talk again soon."

I did not tell Dad about that meeting. Nor did I tell him that he was raising a potential nobody.

"Wanna get something to eat?" I ask Liz after we grab our stuff.

"Yeah, I'm starved." She reaches into her bag and whips out her cell. "Two voicemails. I bet Harry called. He leaves the sweetest messages."

I pull out my cell, just in case. I peer down at the screen. It says I have one message. "Hey, I got a call too!" Dad usually doesn't leave messages, but it could be from Skyler or Anna wanting to update me on their summer adventures.

I hit play. "Hi, Cassia, it's Graham from the gallery. What's up? Call me back. My number's 305-555-2345. *Ciao!*"

I play it again. His voice is so smooth and clear. He could be a Power 96 DJ. I'd love a personal shout-out during the *Love Hour* from DJ Graham.

I can't believe he actually called me. Wahoo! I flail my arms up in the air and do the monkey dance.

Liz doesn't even react. She's on the phone with Harry

now. I can tell by the way her voice has softened to a baby's coo.

I point to my phone and mouth the words, "He called and left a message."

"Really?" She immediately gets off the phone.

We wait for the cars to slow and jet across the street. All the good restaurants are on the other side.

"You didn't have to hang up." I cradle my cell like it has magical powers and orchestrated the phone call from Graham.

"Don't worry. I'll call Harry later—it's not like he's doing anything."

"Wanna hear Graham's sexy voice?" I ask.

"Duh!" Liz holds out her hand.

I bring up the message again and hand over the phone.

"Hi, Cassia, it's Graham," Liz says in a deep, Darth Vader–like voice.

"God, I'm glad he doesn't sound like that." I snatch back my phone. We both laugh.

Liz throws her hands up in the air. "So what are you waiting for?"

"Shouldn't I wait, like, a day to call him back?" We're standing in front of Paloma's Diner. I peer in closer to see if I can catch a glimpse of the grill—my destiny. All I see is a bunch of old guys in suspenders chomping on burgers. This is not a good sign.

"For what?" She shakes her head. "So some other girl can call him?"

"Yeah, I guess you're right. I hate games. But what do I say?"

"Start with hi." Liz laughs.

"Very funny." I bump her with my hip and we keep on walking.

"Ask him about his day. Let him know you're free and he'll take it from there."

The way she says it, it sounds easy. But she's that way with everything. She told me our final history exam was easy after I'd already seen a couple girls from the class before me come out bawling.

"I dunno." I bite my lip.

"Come on! If you don't call him, I'll start singing 'I am Woman, Hear Me Roar.'" She cracks up.

"You would, too."

We park ourselves on the bench at the Number 28 bus stop and I click on Graham's number before Liz can fulfill her dream of singing in public. My heart beats in tandem with the ringing of the phone. Graham answers on the third ring with a hello and tons of bass music in the background.

"Hi, Graham? It's Cassia."

He lowers the volume. "Hey, how's it going?"

"I just had basketball practice."

"That's cool. Who do you play for?"

The bus pulls up and opens its doors. It coughs out a guy in a gray polyester security uniform and takes off.

"Y summer league. What did you do today?"

"Hung at the beach. We wanted to surf but the water was too calm."

We? Dare I ask? "Do you have a lot of surfer friends?"

That was a dork question. It's not like he asked if I had a lot of basketball friends.

"Mostly Jamie and Matt."

Jamie girl? Jamie boy? Oh, this is getting bad.

"What does he want?" Liz whispers.

I shrug my shoulders. What would I do without my life coach?

"Harry and I are going to grab something to eat. Want to join us?" Liz yells in my face, obviously loud enough for Graham to hear.

"Um…" I kick Liz in the shin and she winces. "My friends and I are going to get something to eat—want to come?"

"Can't. My grandparents are coming for dinner. What time will you be home?"

"I dunno. Probably six."

"Where do you live?"

"On Indian Creek Drive. Next to Bay Park." Liz gives me the thumbs-up and pulls out her own phone. Guess I'm flying solo now.

"Is that the building with the funny-colored roof?" Graham asks.

"Yup. Purple power." My claim to fame. I live in a building with a purple roof. You know what they say about purple—ambition, magical power, and strength.

"If you want, I could meet you at your place. Say, eight. I'm not far."

"That works. Call me when you get to the concierge."

"Cool. See ya later." Graham hangs up.

Liz puts her hand over her phone. "Why aren't you jumping for joy? He's coming over, isn't he?"

I didn't realize that a guy bopping to his iPod had joined us at the bus stop. Maybe he's actually waiting for the bus.

"Yeah, but he wants to hang with my dad, breathe in his painterly ways."

"Huh?" Liz stands up from the bench.

I stand up too and walk with her. "That's why he was at the gallery last night."

"Okay." She stops for a minute like her brain's working overtime. "Well, he called you, didn't he? He could've just called your dad straight up."

True.

Right?

notice me yellow

I hardly eat anything at dinner with Liz and Harry. My nerves have gotten the best of me. Graham is coming over in less than an hour!

When I get home, I take a quick shower and spend the rest of the time in my closet. Nothing seems to work and anything I'd usually go for is lying limp at the bottom of my clothes hamper.

It's times like this that it would be great to have a mom to help me with my outfit. If I call Dad in he'll probably tell me to throw on a pair of overalls and a bandana—perfect clothes for painting, not for trying to reel in the guy you're crushing on. I settle on a pair of black short shorts (not short enough to be considered slutty) and a buttercup-yellow T-shirt. The perfect combination of mystery and confidence. It's my *notice me*, not NOTICE ME, outfit.

I walk out into the living room, all freshened up, only

to see Dad watching *Animal Planet* in gym shorts and a cruddy old wine-festival T-shirt. I stand in front of him, blocking his view of the sea lions. "Graham, the guy we met at the gallery last night, is going to be here any minute."

"Oh, great. I picked up a couple of things at the market today. There's ice cream in the freezer. I bought those little Hoodsie cups you like."

"Thanks, Dad. I was hoping maybe you could…"

"You want me to stay out of your way. I get it." He winks at me.

"No, I was hoping you might change. Graham wants to see some of your work."

He points to the TV. "Isn't it amazing how those polar bears stay so white?"

"Dad, I'm serious," I say, arms spread out, now totally blocking his view of the wide screen. "And besides, their fur looks kind of yellowish to me."

He flips off the TV. "Okay, I get the hint. I'll throw on a tux."

"You're the best!" I let out a sigh of relief. "And no smoking, please."

He frowns.

"It's gross and stinks up the place."

"I gotcha," he says, and leaves the room.

I launch into super prep mode. First, I fluff the pillows on the couch, then use the Dustbuster on the coffee table. I light a mango candle in the room to make sure all smells good. Next stop, Dad's studio, because it's supposed to be the highlight of Graham's visit. Just like his official studio, a big open space above La Reverie that he shares with Lucien and another guy named Tony, Dad's mini-studio looks like a typical artist's workshop—paints and brushes strewn everywhere and half-finished canvases stacked against the wall. I dump out the ashtray and open the window for some fresh air.

The phone rings a few minutes after eight. It's security from downstairs. "Cassia, I have Graham Hadley here to see you."

"Thanks, Mitch. Send him up." I love saying that. It makes me feel like I'm sitting in a huge leather chair with my Manolo Blahniks up on the mahogany desk.

I check the foyer mirror. No unidentified objects on my face. No mysterious stains on my clothes. Cleavage. Check. I'm good to go.

A minute later, there's a tap tap on the door. I look through the peephole like I don't know who it is. Graham is even cute in this distorted, magnified, all-about-the-nose view. He's wearing a black T-shirt. So he's game for a little mystery, too.

I unlock the deadbolt. "Hey, Graham. Come in."

"Thanks." He closes the door behind him and slides off his backpack.

We're both standing there in the middle of my foyer. Me with my hands on my hips and Graham with his hands in his pockets.

"So." He looks past me into the living room.

"So." I look into his eyes.

We're both standing here like duh and duh. Then I hear Dad's bedroom door close and his leather sandals inching closer. I can feel him behind me. He rests his hands on my shoulders. "Welcome, Graham." I'm surprised Dad remembered his name.

"Thanks for having me over, sir." Graham holds out his hand.

"Call me Jacques," Dad says, and he and Graham shake. "Let me give you a tour," he adds, like we live in Elvis's mansion instead of a three-bedroom, two-bath condo. We bypass our bedrooms and head straight to Dad's studio.

It's the only room in the house painted white. Dad has a few framed pictures on the walls and a photo of me, him, and Mom from when I was about three. It's a really cute snapshot of us at Disney World. I'm holding this huge blob of cotton candy and Mom and Dad are munching on candy apples. I instinctively park myself in front of the photo so Graham can't see it. I'm not ready to share.

I lean back and pick up a kneaded rubber eraser from Dad's drawing table and stretch it back and forth in my hands. Dad told me I was always swiping them when I first learned to walk; he said it took a lot of convincing and some taste testing to assure me they weren't edible. He always had a bunch in his pocket and whenever I got really bored, one would magically appear.

"That's a great painting." Graham points to the recent portrait of me. "Everything about it is so lifelike."

Yes, I'm right here. Any comments about the owner of the body?

"Yes, *ma cherie* is a great subject," Dad says. "Even if she isn't happy sitting still for so long."

"Dad does a portrait of me every year," I tell Graham.

"That's a great tradition." Graham scrutinizes my face—the one on the canvas, not the living, breathing one. "Even your expression is so realistic, like everyone knows what's on your mind."

I hope not. I glance at the little mirror on Dad's desk. Can Graham tell I'm totally lusting after him, that pools of drool are forming at my feet?

Suddenly the room feels very cramped. The three of us in this packed workspace. "Let's go sit down." I lead the way from the studio to the living room.

Dad sits on the love seat and Graham and I plop down on the big couch. Graham immediately focuses on the huge painting of irises on the wall. "That's one of my favorites. I loved it at the exhibit," he says. Oh no, here we go again. Hottie or not, I don't know if I can stand a whole night of this admiration thing.

I pull my feet up under me on the couch. Graham has his elbows on his knees and is listening to Dad talk about his quest for the perfect flower.

"I've spent more money than I care to remember on flowers," Dad says, "but the best flowers are the ones you pick yourself. Just look around when you're taking a walk and you'll find that beauty surrounds you."

That statement is pretty fitting, especially since we live on Miami Beach where tanned bodies and fashion firsts strut by our doorway every day. It's funny when I see the purple top of my condo building panned over on the E channel or blockbuster movies.

"Yeah, I've been really into landscapes lately. Actually, I'm working on the view of the ocean from my grandparents' condo. They live in Boca."

"Nothing beats an ocean view." Dad fiddles with a stack of plastic drink coasters. "Cassia draws, too."

"Not that much," I interject, eraser still in my hand. That passion is clearly marked *Dad*. Besides, my sketchbook is starting to grow cobwebs. I haven't drawn anything in at least a month. Even then, most stuff never sees the light of day. I mostly draw when I'm bored. I used to draw whole pictures just so I could erase everything on the page. I'd try to get the page as clean as possible without ripping the paper. It was kind of like a game.

"She's spending her time on the court this summer," Dad says, like I'm not even here.

"Yeah, I'm having a lot of fun, too. We won our first game." I fashion the eraser into a circle.

Dad throws an air ball. "Watch out Michael Jordan."

"Dad, he doesn't even play anymore." I frown.

"I love watching old footage of him, though," Graham butts in. "He's a master on the court."

"You play ball?" I ask.

"Oh, yeah. I like watching more, though. I'll watch pretty much any sport on TV, except for bowling." He laughs. "Surfing is my thing. Well, besides art," he adds.

"Surfing looks like a lot of fun. Is it hard to get up on the board?" I stretch my legs out. They're beginning to get numb.

"It takes a few tries, but once you get the hang of it, it's pretty easy. I'll teach you sometime if you like."

"Really?" That would involve me gawking at Cute Butt shirtless in a bathing suit. "Okay, cool."

You hear that, Ms. Cable? That would be two new activities in less than two weeks!

Dad leaps up from the couch with a smile. "I'll be right back."

Oh, no! Anything but the *Time* magazine collection. If he pulls that out, I'm doomed. He inherited it from his Great Aunt Celine. She left his brother and sister cool things like furniture and antiques, but all Dad got was the magazine collection because she said he'd know what to do with it. He stuck it in a crate in the linen closet, that's what he did with it, and pulls it out whenever someone new comes over. No one ever looks at the collection more than once. By the second visit they focus on Dad's works or venture out onto the balcony.

Every few seconds I peek around the corner to make sure he's not dragging that old musty crate across the tile floor. Graham must think I'm a paranoid freak.

Dad comes back a couple minutes later with two Hoodsie cups and spoons. "Ice cream, anyone?"

Okay, I guess I can handle the little kids' birthday party food. Anything is good after the thought of the dreaded magazine collection.

"I love these things." Graham reaches for the small cup. Maybe he's just being polite, but he downs his before I can even get a second bite in. Dad immediately brings him another one, then says, "Will you two excuse me for a while? I've got some paperwork to do." Which translates to, he better send some invoices out or he'll never get paid, then the bills won't get paid either. He's gotten better ever since our electricity was shut off a few summers ago. It was such a pain in the butt. We had no a/c and had to stay at Lucien's for the night.

Now I always open the bills and put them in order for him. There are some amenities I can't live without: a/c, water, and food. At the top of Dad's list would be canvases, paint, and cigarettes. After college he and a friend once lived in a tent in Key Largo for almost four months. Not my idea of fun.

I throw away our Hoodsie containers and bring Graham a glass of water. It's just the two of us sitting on the couch in my condo. It's nice.

The only other guy I've ever had at my place is Zach, my ninth grade science partner and apparently another fan of my dad's. Zach overheard Dad singing "Yellow Submarine" one night when we were on the phone. Turns out

Zach was a Beatles fanatic and actually thought my dad had a decent signing voice. Lucky me, Zach called the next afternoon when I was out and Dad invited him to dinner. Talk about invasion of privacy. By the time I got home, Zach had already toured my house, including my bedroom, and was eating chips and salsa at the kitchen table with Dad. Graham's definitely a step up. He doesn't suck on his retainer or carry a magnifying glass in his back pocket. No offense to Zach, of course.

"Thanks for having me over." Graham pulls a fish-shaped coaster from the stack, slaps it down on the coffee table, and settles his glass on top of it.

"It's nothing." I shrug.

"You're really laid back, not like most girls," Graham says. "I like that."

If he only knew how I fell asleep dreaming about him, had Liz play sleuth and look him up in the yearbook, and spent thirty minutes rummaging through my closet searching for the perfect outfit.

"Thanks." I smile. "I try." This is the point where Liz would say, *Jump his bones, move in for the kiss*. The very same point where I'd say, *For one thing, my dad is in the next room, and for another thing, Graham never said anything about being even remotely attracted to me.* So I do the only passive-aggressive thing I can think of and let down my ravishing light-brown hair (at least the new conditioner I used said it would look ravishing). It's damp and wavy, so it looks extra thick. For all I know, he's not a hair man, but I'll give it a try. I flip it back with my hand and move slightly closer to him. "So what classes are you taking in the fall?"

"Besides the required stuff? Graphic Design and Intensive Art."

"What's that?"

"Kind of something I designed myself and had to get approved by the department head, Mr. Rogan. It's like being an artist's apprentice. Learn from a master and produce a series of pieces by the end of the semester. I figure it's best to get started this summer while I have more time."

I glance at his legs hoping he'll move in closer to me, but he doesn't budge. "Sounds interesting," I say, a second before I realize what's coming next.

"Yeah, I'm really lucky they approved it. I had to write a five-page paper on my goals and what I expect to achieve from doing the study. Mr. Rogan is no joke."

I would have so failed that assignment. I'm having trouble finding just one personal goal.

"Wow, I wish I was doing something cool like that."

Oops, I shouldn't have said that aloud. Now I sound more boring than ever. If he ever finds out that my resume is almost blank, he'll probably stop talking to me.

"You could. You can." He sits up straight. "They approve a lot of things as long as you can show it has *educational merit*." He makes imaginary quotation marks in the air and laughs. "A friend of mine is really into astronomy and is doing this whole project with some famous astronomer guy. Kale, I think his name is."

"So, you want me to ask my dad if he can be your mentor?" I say. I should add some requirements to the mentorship…You have to sleep over every weekend, date the mentor's daughter, and carry a photo of her around in your wallet. Hee hee.

"Well, ah…" Graham shuffles in his seat. "That would be awesome, but I don't want to impose."

Something about him being all nervous turns me on even more. I wonder if Graham has any clue how cute he really is. He must. I'm sure girls are all over him. He probably travels with a posse that rushes him to and from classes.

I get up from the couch. "Stay here. I'll be right back." I walk over to Dad's studio and open the door. He's printing out invoices and stuffing them into envelopes.

"Is your friend still here?" Dad asks.

"Yeah, that's what I wanted to talk to you about." I lean against his chair. "He wants to know if he could study with you. He's doing some directed-study thing for school and he's got to put in a certain number of hours working under a professional. He's in the art magnet."

Dad looks up. His brown eyes are big and round. They look like frying pans. I run my finger over the lids of my own round eyes. Are mine that big?

"Me, a professional?" he asks.

We both laugh. "Yeah, you, Dad."

"What do you think?" He licks an envelope shut.

My eye catches the Disney photo of us again. Mom's smiling at me. I think she'd like Graham. At least for his initiative. I feel like she'd be proud of me for helping him.

"I think he's really excited about it and he seems like a nice guy. He's a lot different than most guys my age. Definitely more mature." Okay, so I don't want to overdo it, to tell Dad that if I sit next to Graham any longer, I'm going to need a bib. The drool factor is that bad.

"Tell him to come by La Reverie on Monday, around three, and to bring his sketchbook. We'll take it from there."

"Thanks, Dad." I wrap my arms around him.

Dad picks up an invoice from the printer and frowns. "I can hardly read this."

"Change the type size." I lean over him to grab the mouse, then click on Font in the toolbar and select 14. "Now print again."

Dad smiles. "What would I do without *ma cherie*?"

"You'd still be using one of those wall telephones and washing your dishes by hand." I shut the door and walk back to Graham. He's exactly where I left him, playing with a loose thread on the pocket of his pants.

I sit on the arm of the couch and tell him to be at my Dad's studio with samples of his work on Monday at three.

"Really?" Graham stands up.

"Yup." I start to smile but stop abruptly when I realize that my next basketball game is scheduled at the very same time.

"Something wrong?" Graham's eyes move back and forth, surveying my face.

Geez, I'm like an open book. I force my lips to form a smile. "Nothing. I'm sure everything's going to be great!"

"Thanks, you're the best." Graham hugs me.

I hug him back and a tingle rushes through my body. My face rests gently on his shoulder. I push a little closer to his neck and am immediately drawn in by his sensual smell. Wow. I breathe in. I'll call it vanilla rain. One of the purest smells on earth.

Cassia Hadley. Now that has a good ring to it!

mud and blood

"Hi, I'm Cassia Bernard Hadley. Nice to meet you." *On center court we have Number 11, Cassia Bernard Hadley. Cassia Bernard Hadley breaks the world record for balancing a penny on her nose for seven hours and fifteen minutes!*

I have to admit, this Cassia Bernard Hadley gig is working really well for me. It's perfect. Both Graham and I are tall, sixteen, Floridians, and love my dad. Oh, my dad. I can't forget that to Graham, there's no Cassia without Jacques. And there's going to be no Jacques at my game this afternoon.

Dad probably wouldn't be happy watching us play the Brown team anyway, and definitely wouldn't want to see the Gray team on Wednesday. I'll invite him to the game on Thursday instead, when we play Purple (spirituality, peace, and imagination). They're much more his color.

Mid-morning, Dad appears from his bedroom with

an unlit cigarette dangling from his mouth. His first stop is always the balcony to get his morning fix. That was Mom's first stop, too, but her reason was to smell the fresh ocean air, not pollute it. For months after she died, I was afraid to go out on the balcony. I don't know if I was more scared of falling over the railing or actually seeing her ghost standing there in her bathrobe. When Dad would go out, I'd hold my breath (or at least try) until he came back inside.

It wasn't until that next summer that Lucien got me to go out there. He bought me a small pink plastic chair with a butterfly painted on it. He placed it next to one of the big white patio chairs. Then he gently took my hand and led me outside. Even though it was the middle of summer, I got goose bumps and asked him to grab me a sweater. He brought me my fuzzy pink sweater, to match the chair, he said, and kneeled down next to me, wrapping his arm around me. He pointed to the ocean and said, "If you speak to her here, she can hear you." Through the warmth of my sweater, Lucien's arm around me and the beating sun, I told Mom that I loved her with all my heart.

———

I'm lying on the couch, still in my PJs, watching the Cartoon Network. The perfect channel to space out to. I have the little eraser ball in my hand from the other night.

Half a smoke later, Dad comes in from the balcony and plants a kiss on my forehead. "Good morning, *ma cherie*."

"Morning," I say back.

Dad heads to the kitchen. I hear drawers and doors opening, then slamming shut. "Looking through these cupboards, you'd think nobody lives here." He laughs.

Yeah, real funny. I had maraschino cherries for breakfast; some trip he must have made to the market yesterday. Our house is all condiments, no sustenance.

"If you leave me some money, I can pick up a few things this morning," I offer.

Dad strolls back into the living room eating peaches straight out of the can. No utensils. I wince as a trickle of juice dribbles down his chin. "That would be great. I've got a busy day today."

I guess part of that's my fault. I'm the one who set up the date between Graham and Dad. I could've said no.

"Dad, I think Graham's really excited."

"Good. What time is he coming by?"

"You said three." I throw the eraser up into the air and catch it with one hand. Coach Parker did tell us to practice, and she didn't stipulate the size of the ball. To make my efforts more authentic, I use my cup from breakfast as the basket.

"Right, I did. Okay, I have a lunch at one at Café Monsoon. Plenty of time."

I flatten the eraser with my palm. "A date? While I'm left home foodless."

"It's with a couple of guys from the bank. Their treat. I suppose you could come."

As long as the blond lady's not eating a jumbo steak

while I'm lugging home groceries from the market. "Nah, I'm fine." Besides, if I'm even going to consider basketball as my passion, I need to spend more time practicing. I fashion the eraser back into a ball and continue shooting.

Dad pulls some bills from his wallet and sets them on the coffee table. "That should cover the basics, and there's an extra twenty in case you want to go to the movies with your friends."

I'm five for five with the baskets. I move the paper cup a little farther away so I can work on my three-pointers. "Thanks, Dad. But I've got a game today."

"Well, maybe afterwards, then." Dad goes to shower and I blast the volume on the TV. I pretend it's the crowd going wild during my exhilarating paper-cup basketball game. The stands are full. Dads are yelling *Go for it!* and moms are clapping so hard, their hearts are popping out of their chests.

Everything hinges on this last shot. Ten seconds left on the clock and the two teams are tied. Cassia Bernard Hadley has control of the ball. She runs down the court, eyes the basket, and…shoots! Ladies and gentlemen, she knocks the basket over by the sheer force of her shot. The refs call it a freak act of nature and demand a replay. This time the basket is reinforced by an empty glass of lemonade that can withstand winds upward of 130 mph. Cassia focuses her eyes on the basket and releases the ball. Ladies and gentlemen, we have a superstar in the making!

I finally get up from the couch around lunchtime

and head for the grocery store. It's always limiting when I shop by myself because I can't carry much home. I pick up some bread, milk, cereal, spaghetti, and marshmallows and call it a day.

My basketball garb is on way before three, so I laze around on the couch until it's time to leave. I hope I don't run into Kate and Zoey again; I'm not in the mood for their crap. I walk fast, past the shops and restaurants, past the beachgoers and bike messengers. No time to even look at wacky tourists as they whiz by. I just want to get out on the court and hustle. I've got to really focus on the ball today so I don't lose control. Coach told us during the first practice that nothing beats determination. Where does she gets this stuff? Did she read it in a self-help book? Or is it from years of coaching?

I'm ready to give it my all today. Whatever that is…I'm not really sure. I spot Liz crossing the street and speedwalk to catch up to her. "Hey, girl, wait up," I yell.

She turns around. "I thought I smelled you."

"Ha, funny. It's probably your new perfume."

She sticks her armpit in my face and makes sniffing noises.

"It's you." I laugh. "Is Harry coming to the game?"

"He wanted to, but then he'd have to get off work early. I told him to come on Thursday instead. That's his day off. What about Graham?"

"What about him? After he meets with my dad today,

the game will be over." I hit the walk button and wait for the little man to appear.

"Come on, coast is clear." Liz pulls my arm and we dash across the street.

"Yeah, I guess it's better to get hit by a car than be late for a game."

"Hey, do you want to run extra laps?" Liz is a few feet in front of me. She swings open the court gate.

Coach is over on the grass talking to some parents and a few girls are already doing their stretches. The Brown team has gathered at the other end of the court. As far as I can see, they don't have any players as tall as Thunder or Zoey.

Liz and I spread out on our side of the court with the rest of the Red team. We're finished with the jumping jacks when Zoey and Thunder arrive. Joy to the world!

Coach joins us on the court. "Good, everyone's here. Finish your stretches, then grab a ball and practice your shots."

Wait a minute—did she not notice that the Amazons were late? How unfair!

We all line up, but Thunder cuts in front of me. "What's the rush, chica?" Liz asks.

"Well, excuse me," Thunder barks back.

"Damn right, excuse you." Liz clicks her tongue.

"Go ahead, Kate," I say, hoping to avoid an all-out cat fight.

"Now, she speaks." Kate looks me dead in the eye.

I think she has smoke coming out of hers. I guess that makes me the fire extinguisher.

I hold my hands out to either side in case one of the cats decides to pounce. "It's really no big deal guys."

Coach walks up to us. "Is there a problem, girls?"

"No," I mumble.

Kate hisses, but then grabs a ball, runs up, and shoots. She misses and slams the ball on the ground.

"Cool it, Kate," Coach yells after her. "Don't make me bench you for the game."

"Don't let that psycho chica intimidate you," Liz says to me once Coach is out of earshot.

"Yeah, you're right." I reach for a ball. "She's getting on my nerves with that 'tude." I know that if I just said the word, Liz would threaten her with a barrage of insults in Spanish and her evil stare, but I don't want her to fight this battle for me. Instead, I'm going to do what I usually do: try and ignore the Thunder beast and hope she goes away.

"Keep it moving," Coach yells.

I quickly run down the court. I pretend the ball is Thunder's head and throw it hard. It bounces off the rim, but I give "Thunder" a good slam.

We practice shooting until Coach calls us over for a team huddle. I make sure to stay away from Thunder and so does Liz. Coach is sporting a brand-new Nike outfit with spandex shorts. She looks like that tennis player Serena Williams. Her legs are ripped.

We pile our hands together inside the huddle and Coach says, "Strong defense today. Keep your eyes on the ball." We finish up with, "Pride!" The huddle folds and the starting lineup assembles.

Liz, Kate, Maria, Zoey, and Teri make up the fabulous five today. One wrong move from Thunder and she'll be struck by Lightning Liz. Liz definitely has balls, but she'd never risk being thrown out of a game.

The ref blows his whistle and the Browns and Reds become one mesh of color. Mud and blood. By the middle of the first quarter, Mud is up by four points. Some of those girls are really built. Their center looks like she has coconuts for calves. I wonder if they double as a wrestling team.

Lightning Liz moves fast with the ball. She avoids the Thunder and passes off to Zoey. Zoey scores again and again. The Browns are fierce, though, especially Number 20, who plows through anyone who gets in her way. I keep my eyes on them, trying to learn their secret. By the time the first-quarter buzzer goes off, I realize there's no secret—they're just that good. The score is 16 to 10, Browns in the lead.

I'm in and out during the second and third quarters. The game is tight at the end of the third quarter. Browns are up by four. I only make one basket, but I hustle like Coach said. I don't give the Browns the opportunity to steal the ball from me, and I make a couple of decent passes.

Liz's mom cheers me and Liz on. It's nice to hear her boisterous voice over all the unfamiliar ones. The Browns have a lot of support. They even have a cheering squad of little girls in Brownie uniforms. I don't know if it was planned, but it does seem very appropriate. It would be kind of hard to get the Red Cross or the wait staff at TGI Friday's to show up as our supporters.

Fourth quarter, I'm in with five minutes left in the game. Browns in the lead, 32 to 28. Coach says we can still beat them.

"Eyes on the ball, girls," she yells from the sideline. I watch the orange circle move back and forth. Teri has the ball. I need to let her know I'm open. This is my chance to score big. My elbows are flexed back and I make like a brick wall, guarding Number 20.

"Over here, Teri." I wave my hands back and forth like I'm a damsel in distress in one of those old black-and-whites that Lucien has us watch every Christmas. I should've invited Lucien to the game. He would've showed, even if he had to leave Monica in charge of the gallery. I peer out into the crowd. There are a lot of fresh faces; I'm sure most of them are for the Browns.

Teri tosses me the ball and I hold on tight. I look left, then right, planning my next move.

A couple of guys yell, "Pass, Eleven." Eleven, that's me. I look over by the huge oak. There are two guys. One is big and beefy and the other is…no, it can't be. The one with the blond spiky hair looks like Graham. I'm pretty dehydrated, so it could be that my mental status has been compromised.

"It's all you, baby," the beefy guy yells, and Spiky Hair says, "Go Kate!"

What? He knows Kate by name? Graham knows Kate.

Bam! I'm knocked to the ground and the ball rolls away. Ouch, that hurt. I blindly reach for the ball, but somebody grabs it and what seems like a herd of elephants stampedes by me.

I'm wide open again, but now the whole team is at the other end of the court…watching the Browns score…a three-pointer. How did that happen? And the whistle blows…Coach calls for a time-out. Isn't anyone going to help me up? I look around. My fellow teammates are all gathered over by the bench. I get up and hobble over to them. Coach stops talking and turns to me. "Are you all right?"

I look down at my legs. My left knee is red. But no blood. "Yeah, I'm fine."

"Good to hear. But what were you thinking? Eleven out, thirty-two in." Coach shakes her head.

So much for sympathy.

"Idiot cost us three points. No chance of winning the game now." Thunder kicks the side of the bench, narrowly missing my leg. No one answers her, but no one springs to my defense either.

The ref blows the whistle and the players are back in position. Four minutes left in the game. Browns are up by seven.

"Are you okay?" Liz taps me on the shoulder, but before

I get a chance to answer, she sprints to the court. She quickly scores a shot and everyone cheers. We're only behind by five now. Miracles can happen.

I remember the potential Graham sighting. Now I really hope it's not him. He's leaning against the tree, with the big guy partially blocking him. Besides, the big guy really doesn't look like someone Graham would hang with. He has his arms crossed and a sneer on his face. I hope that sneer's not meant for me.

"Oh, damn," I hear someone yell. The Browns have stolen the ball and Number 12 is dribbling furiously up their side of the court. Thirty seconds left on the clock. The Reds are not going to come out alive. But wait—Thunder steals the ball, passes off to Teri. Ten seconds left on the clock, and…Teri scores. The buzzer sounds and people are cheering, but it's the Brown team that won, 35 to 32.

I don't want to face my team, so I walk over to the tree instead. I'm about five feet away when I get a really good glimpse of the two mystery guys. Definitely not Graham. But still I stand there, mouth gaping. I'm not sure what just happened.

Someone pushes me from behind. "Thanks for screwing up the game, Cashew."

Ugh, it's Thunder again. "It was only one shot."

"Yeah, the shot that cost us the game. Stay home next time if you want to take a nap." She pushes me again and runs off toward Beefy Dude.

"Bitch," I say when she hits the outer edge of the court, out of earshot. I watch as she hugs the guy and high-fives Spiky Hair. Thank God, it's not Graham. But I take one good look at his butt just to make sure.

I walk over to the side of the court to collect my bag and try not to make eye contact with anyone else. No need to tell me how much I sucked. I already know. I almost trip over Coach's foot when I walk past the bench, which is pretty stupid considering the size of her boats.

She stops talking to Maria and turns to me. "You sure everything's okay, Cassia?"

"Yeah, I'm really sorry. Everything's fine," I say to her Nikes.

She pats me on the back. "Go home and clear your mind. I want you back tomorrow for practice refreshed."

I lower my head. "Coach, I promise I won't space out again." All I had to do was pass or shoot the stupid ball, but instead I totally zoned out.

"You did some good hustling out there today. Just need to keep your focus."

I nod and take off to meet Liz over by the gate. She has her cell glued to her ear. For once I really wish she would get off the phone. I haven't talked to her since my big screw-up exactly twelve minutes and twenty seconds ago.

"Let's get out of here." I tug her arm.

She gets the picture, makes a kissy sound into her phone, and hangs up. "Are you okay?" she says again.

"Yeah. Why does everyone keep asking me that?" I walk toward the crosswalk, but Liz pulls me back.

"My mom's bringing the car around. You just seemed kind of out of it at the end."

"So apparently I'm transparent. I know it's stupid, but I thought I saw Graham."

"My mom has pills for that stuff." Liz laughs.

"This is no time for jokes. I thought the spiky-haired guy with Kate's scary-looking boyfriend was Graham."

Liz sticks her finger in her mouth and makes a gag noise. "You're right. That's no joke. And her boyfriend does kind of look like an ex-con. Don't worry, Graham would never hang out with a toad like her."

"How would you know?"

Her mom beeps her horn and waves. "Go to the gallery and see if he's still there," Liz says. "Wanna ride?"

Maybe I should walk. I need to clear my head, let off some steam. Plus, the last thing I need is one of Liz's pep talks: *You can do it, Cass. Keep your head in the game.* I don't need a second coach. One is enough.

"No, I'm fine. Thanks, though."

Liz hops in the car and holds her fingers up like a phone and mouths, "I'll call you."

Yeah, but not before you call Harry back, I think.

golden shower

Half a block from the gallery, I realize I'm still wearing my sweaty polyester basketball uniform. Red, no longer the color of victory; rather, the color of temper and anger. After all, red attracts raging bulls (Thunder). My psychology teacher, Ms. Kravitz, said it's no coincidence that one of McDonald's official colors is red. Studies have shown that red stimulates the mind and sucks people in. My theory about the game: the red shirts of our team lured the dull browns in and allowed them to soar to victory.

I'm standing in front of La Reverie now, too tired to turn around, go home, and shower. Actually, I'm hoping Graham is long gone and I can talk to Dad. Alone. I could really use a hug right now. When I was little and came home from school with a frown on my face, Dad would pull out two huge blankets. We'd cuddle up on the couch until he put a smile back on my face.

I finally step inside the gallery and stand at the entrance. The cold air is a welcome change from the extreme humidity of Miami summers. I check for *Lady in Red*; she's still there. A smile instantly spreads across my face, and if I squint my eyes, it feels like she's smiling back at me. For all I know she could be asleep under those shades, but I like to think she's looking beyond the canvas.

Then I head upstairs to Dad's studio. I hear them before I see them. Dad and Graham. Talking. Laughing. Talking. Laughing. Aren't they supposed to be working? What time is it, anyway—five thirty? Shouldn't Graham be dust by now?

Dad sees me first. "Ay, Cassia, *ma cherie*, how are you?"

"You had a game?" Graham asks.

Yeah, don't remind me.

I look at Dad, not Graham. "Yes. We lost."

"Sorry," both Graham and Dad gasp, like they're Siamese twins sharing one brain.

"Yup," I say, still frozen in the doorway. All the lights are turned on and the studio has an unfamiliar brightness to it. Everything here is communal, so you would never know that three people share this loftlike space. There are easels spread about, a table and chairs in the back, a large cabinet and boxes of paint and supplies in every corner. Lucien's half-finished painting of a marina is perched on an easel by the door.

"Tell me about it," Dad says.

I shake my head. "It was really crappy…"

Dad holds up his pointer finger, signaling me to hold on, and turns to Graham. "Now I remember the name of the Russian artist. It's Malevich. See if they have anything on him at the library."

Graham just nods.

"Thanks for asking, Dad," I grumble, and walk toward his desk in the back.

"Sorry, *cherie*, please continue."

"Nevermind." I position myself against the wall instead, away from them. "So how was it *here*? At the gallery?"

"Graham's building an impressive portfolio." Dad pats him on the back. "He's got a great eye for detail."

"That's nice," I say, and really mean it until I remember my not-so-great attention to detail. Apparently, I wouldn't even know a basketball if I was holding one in my hand. No, I was too busy mistaking Thunder's friend for Graham. That's like mistaking prune juice for Coke, which, by the way, I only did once.

I think Graham senses I'm an emotional wreck; either that or my high rate of perspiration sends him running because he asks if we have any water. Dad directs him downstairs to the mini-fridge and I take a seat on the paint-splattered footstool.

With my elbows pressed against my thighs, I let out a huge sigh. Desperate times call for desperate measures.

Dad pulls up another stool and sits facing me. "I'm sorry. I know how you feel."

I lift my head. "You do?"

"Of course. I told you the other day I wanted to come. And I bet all the other parents were there, too."

His face is peppered with tiny whiskers. He can't go one day without shaving.

"Don't worry about it. I sucked anyway. Messed up an important play."

He leans in closer and squeezes my arm. "You don't have to tell me. I'm really sorry. I'll come to the next game. I promise."

I hear footsteps on the staircase. Graham's back with a bottled water. "Everything's fine, Dad," I say, and get up from my perch.

"Good to hear." He stands up, too.

I feel like crying. I cost us the game, and I need to curl up on the couch under heavy blankets even though its eighty-five degrees outside. Sure it was only one shot, but why did it have to be THE shot?

I look over at Graham, sketchbook tucked under his arm and a permanent smile tattooed on his face. How can I throw a hissy fit when someone else is so genuinely happy? I can't. That's not me.

"I've got to run. I didn't realize it was so late. But thanks so much, Mr. Bernard, ah, Jacques. I'll be here at ten tomorrow," Graham says.

"My pleasure." Dad reaches out to shake his hand.

Then Graham turns to me. "I'll see you later, Cassia."

My body perks up. "Okay, great," is all I can think to say. But then my shoulders quickly slink down into hunch mode. Of course he's going to see me later. That's like stating a fact. The sky is blue. I look like crap today. I'll see you later. Graham's got what he wants now. Full access to my dad.

He leaves, and I wait for another half hour until Dad finishes up a small canvas he was commissioned to paint for a friend. It's a painting of the guy's Nemo fish. Fish don't count as portraits, apparently. Plus, money talks. I don't know too many people willing to shell out a grand for a picture of their fish. What's next, a still life of the guy's toaster?

I don't even want to think about going to practice tomorrow and facing everyone. I'm such a moron. From now on I'm not going to look at anything but the ball. Maybe I should wear horse blinders.

I play the scene over in my head. Teri has the ball, can't move due to overload of Browns. Cassia is open. Cassia waves her arms wildly to proclaim her freedom, and catches the ball. Cassia thinks of Dad (always him), turns for a split second to the oak tree, mystery man is standing there shouting "Pass, Eleven!" Cassia falls into a deep hallucination and thinks mystery man is Graham. With her mind elsewhere, Cassia gets slammed by a Brown and drops the ball, causing damage to her already compromised brain. Now if only I can convince my team that cerebral injury is the most likely explanation of the events that unfolded.

"Why so blue, kiddo?" Lucien pulls up Dad's stool and sits beside me. He's wearing a cream-colored linen shirt and suit pants. He looks funny sitting on a small, paint-splattered stool. There's something on the corner of his shirt. Looks like a ketchup stain.

"Tough game today," I pout. I watch as Dad walks over to the sink to dump the cup of cloudy paint water. "We lost."

"Nobody likes to lose," Lucien says.

Exactly. Maybe I should've said to Ms. Cable, "What's better, a nobody or a loser? Is it better to be a blip on the radar or a blop?" Okay, so blop is not an actual word, but it sounds like one big mess. Like a blown-up blip.

"It's even worse when it's all your fault," I grumble.

He puts his arm around me. "All *your* fault? Impossible. You can't carry the weight for the entire team."

"Yeah, but I lost the ball and blew a very important shot," I say to his shirt. You really have to work hard to keep linen clean. It picks up everything. Even the hairs from Lucien's cat, Café.

"Then you go out tomorrow and show them what Cassia's really made of," he says.

I pull back a little and look at his face to see if he's serious.

"Do you think I'm going to let one tiny spot ruin my whole outfit?" He holds up the corner of his shirt. "I doubt your coach would, either."

I laugh. "But you should see the way Ms. Parker dresses. She's no joke."

"And neither are you." Lucien gives my shoulder a tap and helps me up.

Dad sprays his painting with matte finish, and the aerosol smell quickly fills the air. I cough.

He gathers his stuff. "Ready to go, *cherie*?"

"She's ready." Lucien smiles at me.

———

Dad and I pick up takeout for dinner from Pasta Genie and eat in front of the TV. We end up twirling our spaghetti and watching *Deal or No Deal*, which turns into a conversation about what we'd do with the prize money. European travel is on both of our lists, surfing lessons for me and a new studio for Dad. We both agree a maid would be nice, too.

After the show, an ad comes on for the Miami Heat.

"We should go to a game sometime," Dad suggests.

"Sure. That'd be fun." If it would ever really happen.

Dad gathers the dishes. "What got you interested in basketball, anyway?"

"Well, I felt like doing something physical this summer, so I asked my P.E. teacher if he knew of a place I could play and he suggested the Y. He said I'm a good ball player." I fold up the extra napkins.

"That's great. It's a good game," Dad says.

I can't tell him I'm on a passion-seeking mission. He was practically born with a paintbrush in his hand. He'd never understand.

After dinner I call Liz, but her voicemail picks up. I'm sure she's with Harry. I flip the channels on the TV in my room but nothing grabs me. There are only so many matchmaking and self-help shows that one can take. Maybe a book will keep me occupied. I always find something good to read from the bookshelf in the living room. As I run my hands over the bindings, I see the book Mom made. Well, it's not really a book, but a collection of pressed flowers bound into a scrapbook. I grab a copy of *Of Mice and Men* and the pressed flowers and head back to my room. I open Mom's book first and run my fingers over the crinkly paper. Next to each flower she wrote the common name, scientific name, and its origin.

The first one is an *Amaryllis belladonna* or, as I like to refer to it, the Naked Lady. It's from San Diego. The stem has no leaves and the pink petals are spread pretty wide apart. I wonder if my mom ever visited California. It's a place I've never been, but I can imagine the naked ladies strutting their stuff; not much different than South Beach, really!

On the next page is a more subtle flower, the lemon bacopa or, scientific name, *Bacopa caroliniana*. It has four purplish-blue petals and a yellowish center. I flip past the bladderwort, African violet, and marigold and go right to my favorite, *Cassia fistula*, a native of South Florida. It's hard to believe Dad named me after a plant in the pea family, but circumstance prevails. He first saw Mom when she was standing in front of the plant, waiting for a bus. He was eighteen, barely out of high school, and she was sixteen. I should be thankful they didn't name me after the naked lady or the bladderwort. The common name for this yellow plant, with small delicate petals, is golden shower.

Naturally, when I learned my name's meaning, I thought it meant a shower of pure gold. However, about five years later, a psycho kid in my fourth grade class, Allen Farnsworth, told me a golden shower is when you piss all over someone because you really like them. I thought he was a total liar until he asked if I wanted a demonstration. I didn't stay past him unzipping his fly, but cried all the way home. I couldn't pee for the rest of the night. My dad was sure I had a bladder infection. He bribed me with a trip to the toy store the next day if I went to the bathroom. It worked. Needless to say, I haven't shared the secret meaning of my name with anyone. Not even Liz.

I stare at the yellow flower, trying to see what Dad saw when he first laid eyes on Mom. I bet the golden yellow flower was the perfect backdrop to her ink-black hair. She probably wore it loose, like she does in most of the pictures. I don't think I live up to her. How could I? She was the love of his life.

colorless

Dad wakes me up at nine to go to the gallery. He never gets up that early, but he promised to meet Graham for a couple hours before his lunch date with a potential buyer. I don't see what I'm going to do there while they're talking shop, but it's not like I have anything to do at home, either. I can't stare at Graham's butt the whole time, so I stock my bag with a magazine, pencils, erasers, and a mini-sketchpad.

I'm really not in the mood to think about my outfit. I just throw on a white T-shirt and khaki shorts. It's one of those days following one of those nights, I can feel it. Liz didn't even call me back yet. *Wench.*

As Dad and I make our way down Collins Avenue to the gallery, we pass a men's store with a gray suit in the window. I know it's designed to make a man appear powerful, but standing alone, it looks so drab. I can't help but wonder what if all the storefronts were gray. If the clothing racks were only filled with white shirts and gray pants. A futuristic science fiction society where everyone wears the same thing. Extracting color is like removing parts of people's personalities. A world void of color is like a world void of individuality. Okay, I know color does not make you who you are, but it helps express how you feel. And right now I feel blah to the core.

———

Surprise, surprise, Graham's already waiting for us at La Reverie. The place opens at ten, so Dad goes ahead and lets us in. Graham's carrying an oversized portfolio case with him. What's next? A moving truck filled with everything he's drawn since preschool?

Dad grabs us a few waters from the mini-fridge and we trudge up to the studio. There's a table and chair toward the back of the room, so I set myself up there. Dad pulls out a couple of folding chairs from the closet and sits with Graham in front of the easels.

"Feel free to join us anytime, Cassia. I can set you up with an easel, too." Dad goes back to the closet to grab more supplies.

"Thanks," I say, flipping open the latest issue of *People* Magazine. Some of these celebs are pretty hot and scandalous. I'm especially digging the shot of the Ed Hardy model on the beach with no shirt on. Yum, yum.

I glance over at Graham. He's wearing an everyday, navy blue pocket-tee. I can only dream about what he's got hiding under there. He is a surfer dude after all, so I bet he's ripped. Now if I had my x-ray glasses with me, I could snag a better look.

Graham has this swirly, abstract, bold-colored painting balanced on the easel. He's used colors I would've never thought to put together, but somehow they work. Bright reds and deep purples, with a thin line of brown. He's explaining the image to Dad, telling him how it was painted during a really bad tropical storm. I wonder how long I have to stare at Graham in order for him to think I'm a wacko. I make sure to look away every few seconds, but my eyes keep diverting back to him. There's something so genuine about the way he talks, even his gestures. He's all smiles for every sample he shows Dad. He doesn't make excuses for any of his pieces, like "this one is not my best"…no, everything is his best.

I'm totally checking Graham out when he shouts, "Hey, Cassia, what are you working on back there?"

I quickly shut the magazine and pull out my sketch pad. "Nothing much yet. Still getting started."

"Can I take a look at nothing when you're done?" He laughs.

"Absolutely," I say.

I pull out a pencil and flip to a blank page. I don't know what to draw. In classes I doodle happy things like butterflies or flowers, but I'm not in the mood today.

My sixth grade art teacher, Mrs. Francis, always said if you don't know what to draw, think of what you really want. At the time I wanted a new bike, so I started with that. It wasn't the easiest thing to draw with the spokes and all, so I told Mrs. Frances I changed my mind and drew a scooter instead. I know it's a cop-out because I already had a scooter, but I still got an A.

What do I want? More sleep. Maybe a new haircut. A passion to call my own. Time alone with Graham. Graham. Yeah, I could draw him, but his back is to me. Not that I'm complaining.

My pencil hits the page before I can change my mind. I sketch Graham's backside from the waist down. I hardly have to look up because I already know his ass by heart. I'm glad he chose a pair of jean shorts today instead of his baggy cargo pants—the pockets on those things really take away from his natural shape. I can't let my imagination do all the work.

I use the eraser only for shading. Otherwise, I'm pretty happy with the way the drawing is coming out. I should do a whole series on people's derrières. If I get well-known, maybe celebrities will fly me in to sketch their behinds. Or the whole thing could backfire and I could be known as That Creepy Butt Girl!

"Lemme take a peek," I hear Graham say, about a foot away from my little setup.

"What?" I pop up from my butt-induced coma. "At this? No way." I throw the top half of my body over the sketchbook.

Graham's standing next to me now. "I know it's rough."

How did I get myself into this mess? "Not today." Not ever.

Graham holds a small square of paper in his hand. "I'll show you mine if you show me yours."

Huh? And risk being labeled the Psycho Butt Girl? I hover over the book and flip the page.

"Come on, I'm sure it's great." He leans in closer to me.

My shoulders tense up. "No, it's not."

"All I can make out is a heart and…"

I look down at the paper. Damn, why couldn't I have flipped to another page? And why did I have to write *I love Juan*? I haven't loved Juan since he got suspended freshman year for peeing in the cafeteria trash can. However, it can't be as embarrassing as the butt.

Graham's still holding up his piece of paper. On the page is a thumbnail sketch of a stool. I'm going to give up the butt for that? He's got to be crazy.

I'm sweating, and I'm sure my face is bright red.

"It's not much." Graham shifts back and forth. "Just a quick drawing to warm up. We're working on definition today."

"Oh, no, it's a very fine stool," I say, only too thrilled to take the attention off of me.

"You don't have to say that."

"No, I'm serious."

Dad walks back into the studio. "Found the charcoal I was looking for."

"I'll get a look at yours later," Graham says, then joins Dad over at the easels.

Hmmm, we'll see about that. I clench my butt cheeks. I better start doing some toning exercises if I'm going to expose all.

How about a modeling career? Not. It's one thing to sit still every year so Dad can paint my portrait, but to hold a pose to sell a handbag or new frosty lipstick sounds painful. To me it seems devoid of passion because other people are controlling what you do, how you look.

For the rest of the session I don't even dare pull out my sketchbook again. I stick with the known and resume reading my magazine filled with people selling handbags and frosty lipstick. My phone rings as Dad and Graham are talking about their favorite game shows. What that has to do with art, God only knows.

"Hey, Cass. What's up?"

I whisper into the phone, "Liz, where have you been?"

"Why, is something wrong?"

"I can't really talk right now." I crouch down a bit.

"What is it?" I can sense the panic in her voice.

"I'm at the gallery and my dad is with Graham."

"Great. I'll be right up."

"Here? Now?" I come up way too quick out of my crouching position and bump my head on the corner of the desk. "Ouch."

"You okay?"

"Yeah, fine." I rub my head.

"I'm down the street. I had to return a shirt to Old Navy."

Before she even asks, I'm waiting downstairs for her. I don't even bother excusing myself because Dad and Graham are back to work, engrossed in a discussion on definition again.

I quickly pull Liz inside. "So where's Graham?" she asks.

I love Liz to death, but she is loud. "Shhh." I point to the staircase. "I don't want him to hear us."

She looks me up and down, then scrunches her eyebrows together.

"What?" I ask.

"That is no outfit to snag a guy in."

"Who says I'm trying to *snag* him?"

She puts her hand on her hips. "Who are you trying to fool, girl?" She rummages through her Old Navy bag and pulls out a pink tank top. "Here, put this on."

"But he's already seen me in this." I tug on the bottom of my white tee.

"That's what I'm afraid of." Liz shoves the tank into my hands.

There's no use arguing with Liz, so I follow her into the bathroom and throw on the shirt.

"What do you think?" I turn sideways in the mirror and suck in my stomach.

"Much better." She pulls a tube of pink lipstick from her purse and gestures for me to move closer to her. She fills in my lips like she does this every day.

"Isn't this a bit obvious?" I look at myself in the mirror and purse my lips together. *Not bad.* I don't look so washed out.

"Do you want him to notice you or mistake you for a piece of furniture?"

"I was going for the ottoman," I laugh.

"I'm serious." Liz gestures for me to straighten my back.

"All right, I get the point."

Liz lathers her hands with mousse. Then runs her fingers through my hair and fluffs it out. "Now you're ready."

"For what?"

"Just trust me." She leads me back into the gallery and immediately heads for the stairs, but Dad and Graham are already coming down.

"Hi, Jacques." Liz waves to Dad.

"Hello, my dear." Dad smiles.

Graham emerges from behind Dad, but his portfolio case covers half of his body. "Hi," he says.

Liz bops up closer to him. "I'm Liz, Cass's friend. Came to pick her up. We're going to the beach. Want to come? You won't be the only guy. We're meeting my man Harry there." She says this all in one breath, and it actually comes out sounding natural. I think she was one of those door-to-door salespeople in her past life.

"Well, I got this thing." Graham holds up the portfolio case.

Liz looks at my Dad. "So leave it here."

"It'll be safe upstairs," Dad says.

Oh my God, I can't believe he's really coming with us. I hope I don't do anything else stupid.

"Perfect." Graham swings the handle on his case. "I'll be right back."

This makes me nervous. I eyeball Liz.

"Trust me. It'll be fun." She winks at me.

After the whole sketchbook incident I'm really not sure what he thinks of me. He hasn't looked at me. I mean, really looked at me the way I look at him.

I kiss Dad goodbye and the three of us are on our way. We're meeting Harry at the entrance to the beach by the playground.

"I'm so glad we got some color into you." Liz slides her shades on. "Don't you agree, Graham?"

Oh, how embarrassing. I duck my head.

"Yes, that's a very nice color." He blushes.

It takes us about ten minutes to get to the beach and another ten to wait for Harry. We sit on a bench near the entrance and sweat it out. Harry runs up to Liz, throws his arms around her, and gives her a big kiss on the lips.

Their PDA makes me a little uncomfortable, but it doesn't seem to faze Graham. He stands up and introduces himself to Harry. The two high-five like they're old pals. Of course, maybe Graham's an expert in PDA. I'd love to see his relationship resume, but there's no way I'd share mine. It's only two lines long. *Third Grade: Kissed Kevin Smith on a dare. Reward: A box of animal crackers. Eighth*

Grade: Sloppy kissed Franklin Morris at the Valentine's Day Dance. Had to use a napkin to wipe his drool from my face.

We walk down the pathway toward the beach front, weave through a few families and a bunch of girls slathering on suntan lotion before choosing a spot near the water where the sand is damp. This time of year the beach is overrun by tourists, so a place near the water is prime real estate. None of us are dressed for the beach, but we all kick off our shoes and try to squeeze on the one orange towel that Harry brought. Liz and I end up occupying most of it, with the guys on either side of us.

There's a nice breeze over the ocean. I inhale the fresh salt air. Nobody talks. There's a lot to take in. The magnificent view. The cruise ship out at sea, the group of guys playing water volleyball and the mass of sunbathers soaking up the rays at every angle.

A really tan blonde in a black micro bikini sashays by, flanked by an older guy with a hairy chest. Harry does a double take. "Damn, she's fine."

Graham sits up straight to get a better view. "Looks like a super model."

I stretch my legs out in front of me and dig my toes into the cool sand.

"Hey, keep your eyes over here." Liz grabs Harry's chin and brings his face closer to hers.

"Don't worry, babe. Did you see who she was with?" Harry plays with the few wisps of hair that have fallen out of her ponytail.

I scoop up a handful of sand and pack it on top of my feet. "Yeah, he was old."

"Probably her Dad," Liz says.

"Great, then she's a free agent." Harry's eyes light up.

Graham picks up a shell and throws it up in the air. He catches it. "Hey man, you don't want to get between a girl and her father."

He didn't just say that, did he? I look over at Liz. The sand is up to my knees so I can't move, but I plead with my eyes for her to say something to save me. To tell Graham how he is so very wrong. But she doesn't even look my way.

"Yeah, I'll sic my dad on you if you're not careful." Liz pulls away from Harry.

Harry makes a pouty face. "I'm with Graham on this one. Glad I met you first and not your dad."

"That's so sweet," Liz says and pulls the human yo-yo back toward her. "But if you did work at one of my dad's restaurants, I'd make sure he fired your ass, so I could have you all to myself."

So now I have to get Graham fired? The same Graham my dad adores? There is no hope. My legs are completely buried now.

licorice chick

After the beach, Graham runs off to a dentist appointment, so Harry walks us back to my place. I have to endure Liz and Harry's five-minute kiss before he leaves for work. You would think he was leaving for a year in Africa, not a four-hour shift at an ice cream shop two blocks away.

Liz comes inside to get ready for basketball with me, but there's a message on my home phone that practice has been cancelled. It's from a guy at the Y, saying that Coach Parker had to rush her dog to the vet. I never pictured her with a pet. I thought she lived alone with her basketball.

I'm lying on my bed, face down. I lift my head and proclaim to all who care, "I'm doomed."

Liz's standing in front of my mirror and pulls the strap of her tank top down to inspect her tan. "What are you talking about?"

I can feel my blood pressure rising. "That whole thing with Graham about never wanting to date a girl if he knows her dad."

Liz drops her chin and turns to face me. "Oh, that."

"Now what? Somebody save me," I scream into my pillow.

Liz sits down next to me and pats my back. I don't need comfort. I need Graham to like me. "That conversation had nothing to do with you."

"Who else was he referring to? And don't say I have to tell my dad that Graham's an axe murderer and never to let him back in the studio."

"Whoa, calm down, girl." Liz leans back. "I was thinking something else."

"And that something is...?" I can tell she hasn't thought about it, because Liz is rarely at a loss for words.

"You're going to have to make him lust after you," she says.

"I don't know." I shake my head. "Maybe I should just go out with Thomas Dunbar instead."

"The guy that shows up at the gallery just to see how much food he can shove into his mouth?"

"Yes, Monica's nephew. But he does other things too."

"Like?"

"He plays baseball and once I saw him at Starbucks."

"A match made in heaven." Liz throws her hands up in the air and starts cracking up.

"Okay, fine. You win. So how do I get Graham to lust after me?"

She walks over to my desk and pulls out a pad of paper and a pen. "Tell me what he likes."

"Art for one. My dad. Um…surfing…watching sports."

"Well, you're a good artist." She nods like she's trying to convince herself.

"Yeah, I guess, but I'm not going to impress him by hanging my drawings all over the place and he already knows I don't surf."

"But you could if you had to. Right?"

"Are you serious? Surfing is not one of those things you can learn on an emergency basis like driving a car."

"Hmm." Liz nods as if she's in deep thought.

I pull a throw pillow off my bed and hit myself over the head with it. "Let's face it, Ms. Cable was right."

Liz quickly snaps out of her thought coma. "What? You're going to let the lady with the mole on her face and pixie-stick legs tell you that you suck? I've had enough of this woman!"

I stretch out my legs. They aren't exactly short and stubby, but you'd never call them pixie stick, either. "She does have a point. It's a competitive world out there and maybe I'm better off settling before I waste everyone's time and money."

Liz shakes her arms at me. "Settling for what? You have so much talent. I don't know anyone that is as artistic as you."

"Except for one person." I point to one of Dad's daisy paintings above my head.

"Hello, he's your dad and you're his daughter. Where else do we get our talents from?"

"Never thought about it that way," I say. "But it's just that I don't feel like I can ever compare."

"And you're not supposed to. Damn, next time I see Cable I'm going to shake her."

"You're lucky you have Mr. Doug."

"Yeah, he's a real winner." She laughs. "He's usually cleaning out his earwax with a pencil when he meets with students."

I totally crack up picturing the six-foot-five counselor poking a no. 2 into his ear while Liz tries to discuss her future aspirations.

"I've got an idea." Liz whips out her cell and scrolls through her contacts list.

"Oh, no!" I sit up. "Who are you calling? I don't need any more lessons and I'm not up for learning a foreign language now or anything like that."

She doesn't get a chance to answer because the person on the other line picks up. "Can I speak to Deena, please?" She puts her hand over the phone. "I'm trying to get you an appointment for this afternoon."

"For a lobotomy? Don't you need parent permission for that?"

Liz bops up and down like she's trying to shut me up. "Hey, Deena. It's me. Lizzie. You remember my friend, Cassia?

Well, she needs a little help. Can we come by tonight? Cool, you're the best! See ya!"

"Was that your cousin who works at the salon?"

"Yeah, she said come by at seven. I was thinking blond highlights. Something that brings out your features, and…" She scrutinizes my face. "An eyebrow wax."

"Me, a blonde?" I get up and walk toward the mirror. I think of the picture of Mom in our big leather photo album, the one where she's brushing her hair. I like to imagine that she brushed it one hundred strokes every night. I turn around to face Liz. "Black. I want to dye my hair black."

Liz flares her nostrils. "Why? Goth is out."

"I think it'll be a good look for me. That's all." Maybe a fresh start begins from the outside.

"I guess you have to feel comfortable in your own skin."

I hold my arm up to hers. "Looks like we both got some more color today."

"Yeah, I know. My mom's always on my case about using sunscreen and that whole cancer thing, but a girl's got to have a little color."

"I know what you mean." But I really don't. My dad's never on my case about anything. He always mentions that I have a smart head and I know what to do. But how can that always be true? "Let's see what's on TV." I grab the remote and stop on a makeover show.

"Must be karma." Liz laughs.

We spend the rest of the afternoon glued to back-to-back makeover shows on TLC. I certainly know what I don't want to look like.

At six thirty I call Dad to let him know I won't be back until my transformation is complete, but he doesn't answer. I hope he's not on a date, too busy smooching to answer my call. Total gross-out factor. I contemplate not leaving him a message and making him worry about my whereabouts; would serve him right, too. But I don't have the guts to do that. Even if he's the one who dissed my call.

———

I like sitting in this swivel salon chair. It makes me feel important. I'm waiting for my consultation with Deena and watching all the satisfied customers admire their hair-dos as they twirl from side to side in front of the mirrors. Swish, swish goes the chestnut bob. Whoosh, whoosh, goes the blond layered do. Okay, so I have nothing better to do than add sound effects to everyone that walks by.

"What are we looking for today, sweetie?" Deena stands behind me. I can see her in the mirror. Something is different from the last time I saw her. She's straightened her hair, and it's redder now. I want to look different, too.

My eyes meet hers in the mirror. "I want to dye my hair black."

"So dark?" she asks.

"Yeah. I thought about it and that's what I want." I hope.

"I always like a customer that knows what she wants."

Deena picks up a section of my hair. "Who has the nice thick locks? Your mom or dad?"

"My mom. Her hair is really long, too. And black."

Maybe if I dye mine, it'll bring me closer to her. I know it sounds corny, but it's worth a try. I watched a show a couple of years ago about channeling dead people. That if you try hard enough, you can reach them. I set up candles that night and meditated, but no signs of Mom's existence came to me. I thought maybe I wasn't trying hard enough, so the next time I set out pictures of her and sprayed my room with perfume. Still nothing appeared, but I did dream of her that night. She was a mermaid seated on the ocean floor, beautiful as ever. Her skin glowed in the sun and her thick black hair covered her shoulders. I reached out and stroked her hair; it felt like silk. We didn't speak, but we didn't need too. The touch was enough.

"Ah, I see." Deena nods her head.

I look around the room for Liz and spot her at a desk in the corner getting a manicure. She holds up two bottles of nail polish. "Which one?" she mouths.

"Pink," I say. The color of love, relaxation, and contentment. Cotton candy, baby cheeks, and carnations. Not that this pink tank top brought me much luck with Graham today. Maybe the color with a reddish hue will serve her better.

Deena jets off to mix the hair dye and leaves me with a bunch of magazines. I love the crazy, off-the-wall hairstyles that no real person would ever get, but they look cool anyway. The kind where the models wear a lot of shiny makeup and have their hair sticking up in different directions.

Deena's back with a bottle of dye and a bunch of hair clips. She shakes the bottle. "Are you sure?"

Black, the color of mystery, wisdom, and the unknown. Black like the night, lungs of a smoker, and Kalamata olives.

Does she know something I don't? "Fire away," I say, before I change my mind.

The dye stings my scalp, but I don't tell Deena because I'm afraid she'll stop and I'll end up with a striped do. I close my eyes and imagine that I'm Mom. Bianca Bernard. Beautiful. Intelligent. Free.

If I knew how long it took to dye your hair black, I might have reconsidered. I feel like I've been here all night when Deena finally says I can have a seat next to the stack of magazines while we wait for the dye to set in. I catch a glimpse of myself in the mirror and feel like an android, with my hair all clumped together in several different sections. Deena sets the timer for thirty minutes and says she'll be back to check on me. I keep an eye on the clock. I'm afraid she'll forget about me and by the time she remembers, all my hair will have fallen out. Bald is not a fashion option for me.

"How's it going, Vampire Girl?" Liz plops down next to me.

"Could you at least come up with something more glamorous?"

"Sorry." She gives me a long stare. "Licorice Chick?"

"I kind of like that." I hope Graham is the licorice type of guy.

I glance at the time again. Ten minutes left. Deena still hasn't come by to check on me. Maybe she got cold feet and fled the salon.

"You like?" Liz wiggles her fingers and toes.

"Yeah, the coral polish really brings out your tan."

"Thanks." She jumps up from her chair. "I have to call Harry, but I'll be back."

"Okay, fine, leave me here…"

She flips her wrist. "You'll be fine, Licorice Chick."

The timer goes off and I call for Deena. She smells like vinegar salad dressing when she returns. I guess she's got to take a dinner break sometime. She washes out the licorice before I even get a glimpse. Then I'm back in the chair where she claims she's giving me a *chic* do. I can't tell much because my hair's wet, but it's definitely dark.

When she's done snipping, she says, "I'll blow it out for you so you don't have to leave with wet hair."

"Thanks." I could get used to this.

She pulls out a dryer. "Now if you want to stay with the black, you're going to have to come back in three to four weeks so I can touch up the roots."

I just nod. I'm not thinking about what I'll look like in three to four weeks, I'm thinking about what Graham will say when he sees me. Will his eyes drop to the floor? Or will he declare his undying love for me? I wish.

Now Dad, he's another story. Maybe I should've gone blond since it seems like that's his type these days.

"We're all finished." Deena twirls my chair around and hands me a small mirror. "Take a look at the back. It's very full when you blow it out."

I squint because I'm not sure if I can take in the whole transformation at once.

"Very mysterious." Deena smiles. "You like it?"

I purse my lips and tilt my head to the side. There's definitely a strong contrast between my light skin and my rich black hair.

It takes me a long time to answer her, but finally I say yes. I don't want to hurt her feelings. Besides, I think I like it.

"Well?" I twirl in front of Liz once we get outside.

"Wow, your cheekbones really stick out with all those layers."

My mouth drops. "Is that a good thing or a bad thing?"

"Rock star cool," she says. "I didn't think I'd like it, but I do."

"Thanks." I'm still skeptical, though. "Rock star cool as in young and cool or aging rocker dude?"

Liz rolls her eyes. "Do you think I'm going to compare you to an old guy that slurs his words and eats bats?"

We both laugh.

———

Dad's not back yet when I get home, so I scour through all the old photo albums searching for pictures of Mom. My favorite photo is *Bianca and Jacques at a New Year's Eve soiree in New York City*. Mom's wearing an indigo dress and Dad has on a navy suit with a big collar. Dad has his arm firmly planted around Mom like he's her protector.

Bianca. I can imagine Dad saying her name, exaggerating each syllable. *Bee-aaan-caw*. When Graham says my name, it's like he's rushing and all the letters stick together. It comes out like *see-ya*. That always makes a girl feel good. Now why couldn't my parents have named me Olive Juice. If Graham said that nice and slow, I'd melt.

I run my fingers through the underneath of my licorice do. It's still soft, even with the dye job. I wonder if my mom, Bianca, would've approved. "You like, Mom?" I whisper.

I want to know what her name means, so I do a Google search and find a baby name site. Bianca is Italian, meaning white and pure. I push away from my computer and stare into the mirror. Then I remember something Dad always says when he's discussing color. Something very elementary. White reveals. Black conceals. I stare at the black hair of the girl in the mirror. What is she hiding?

the anti-color

It's eleven p.m. when Dad gets home. I'm sprawled out on the sofa reading *Of Mice and Men* and he's laughing hysterically on his cell. The same cell he couldn't answer when I tried to call earlier.

"Oh, Cassia's here," he says to the person on the phone. Not to me.

Was I not supposed to be here?

Dad tosses his keys onto the kitchen counter. "Lucien says good night."

He's talking to Lucien, *phew*. I breathe a sigh of relief. "Good night, Lucien," I say loudly, hoping he can hear.

Dad gets off the phone and joins me on the couch. "What did you do tonight?"

Hmmm, I guess my hair isn't enough of a clue. "I hung out with Liz."

"Did you have fun at the beach?"

"Yeah. Where were you tonight?"

"I didn't tell you?" He cocks his head to the side.

"No, that's why I'm asking."

"I had dinner with Helga. She was at the gallery the other night. Sporty, short blond hair…"

"Helga? Is that her real name?"

Dad throws his hands back. "Yes, why wouldn't it be?"

"Because I didn't think people were really named Helga." I put my feet up on the coffee table. "Yeah, I remember her." *She had her hands all over you.* "Was it a date?"

"Oh, no." Dad tugs his earlobe. "She's an art history professor at University of Miami. Fascinating lady."

"I bet."

Dad grabs my chin. "Sorry, *ma cherie.* I thought I told you I was going out." Still holding my chin, he turns my head to the side. "You look different."

No shit. And he, being an artist, is supposed to have a keen eye. "Yeah, I went to the hairdresser tonight."

"Let me get a better look." Dad turns on the table lamp. One of the few pieces left that Mom bought. It's clear glass and she filled it with shells collected from the beach. I hope it lasts forever. "Black. It's nice. Is that what all your friends are doing?"

"No." I shake my head, thoroughly annoyed. "Just me."

"No tattoos, okay?" Dad laughs.

"Whatever," I mumble. He doesn't even say anything about Mom. About how I look like her now.

"I'm off to bed, *cherie*. I'm going to try and get to the studio early tomorrow. I've got a couple of paintings to finish."

He's behind me now, so I give him the backwards wave. "'Night, Dad."

———

I don't feel like going with Dad to the gallery today. I'm not in the mood to see Graham after he made the comment about not getting between a girl and her dad. Maybe if he doesn't associate me with my dad, I might stand a chance. Changing my last name and getting emancipated is not an option, however.

Anyway, we have a game in the afternoon and I need to put all my concentration into that. I can't mess up today. After Monday's disaster, I have to play really well in order to regain my rep. Not that I had much of one before, but I don't want to be known as the Screw-up Girl.

I get into complete basketball mode and put on my uniform at noon, a full three hours before we're scheduled to be on the court. I scan the channels searching for a WNBA game but can't find one.

What I need most is help focusing. Maybe if I do, I can be a decent player and have people cheer for me, instead of boo.

I hunt down the closest thing to a basketball and come up with an orange. It's starting to mold, but it'll do. I set up a garbage can next to the couch and place the orange on the coffee table. Then I stare at the two objects. Orange.

Garbage can. Orange in the garbage can. I pick it up and throw it in the garbage. It lands with a thud. Score!

I keep on shooting baskets until I'm getting most of them in. The orange is flat after a few minutes, but I don't stop until it starts spraying. I like the pace of home basketball and think I've got an air-tight strategy. Focus being the operative word.

At two thirty I leave my house and walk over to the court. I pass all the usual places. But on the corner of 62 and Collins I notice a small tattoo parlor, John's Tats. I'm sure it's been there for a while, but I've never really taken notice of it. I should go in and get a tattoo just to see how long it takes Dad to register it, but I think you need parent permission to ink yourself.

I hit the walk button and that's when I see trouble walking toward me. If I ever needed the little man to light up, it's now. Sprinting across the street is not an option because cars are whizzing over the bridge.

Thunder's not with Zoey today; instead, she's with the beefy guy from the game. I still can't believe I thought his friend was Graham. This guy looks mean like a bulldog and seems a lot older than us. He's definitely not the type to chit-chat about art. Art to him is probably the picture of Sponge Bob on a Campbell's soup can.

Great, now I have two people to pelt me with verbal darts. This is not something I want to stick around for. The light changes and I motor across the street. My plan is to not look back and hope they ditch into a store or something. I'm walking so fast, all I can hear is the sound of me breathing. I see the delivery trucks and bike messengers coming and going, but I don't hear them. Actually, come to think of it, I don't hear Thunder either. I know she's still behind me because I do hear him. His voice is kind of high for such a big guy. It's like he got a double dose of soprano and was short-changed on the bass. He's saying something about putting a new engine in his car so he can blast past those suckers. Whatever that means. I'm just grateful Thunder's not on my case. It's not like her to give up center court to somebody else. She must really like him, either that or he's more of a stage hog than her.

I can't help myself, and I turn around for a second. Thunder's rubbing his shoulder. His gaze is locked on the pavement now. She catches my eye, drops her arm, and sneers through her smile. I quickly turn back around. I wonder how long they will last together. Adding beefy thunder babies to this world would be a scary thing.

I get to the court, unscathed but severely out of breath, and I see gray everywhere. How sad is that—we're playing the anti-color. The color of sorrow, detachment, and loneliness (old sneakers, chewed gum, and wolves). They could at least call themselves the Silver team—Olympic medals, teapots, and jewelry.

We gather around Coach for some instruction. She apologizes for missing practice yesterday and says she hopes we had the initiative to practice on our own. Then she sends us to run a lap around the baseball field. It wouldn't be such a bad idea if it weren't ninety degrees outside right now.

I head out with Liz. We're moving along at a decent pace, despite having to wipe the dripping sweat from our faces every few seconds. Heat stroke is a definite possibility today. When we get back to the court everyone makes a mad dash for the water cooler.

After downing five cups, I go over to the ball bag to pick out a ball. If I can, I really want to reunite with Baldwin. He was good for practicing shots. I rummage through the bag because they really all look alike. I finally pull one out that I think might be him.

Thunder comes up to me and grins. "Happy Halloween."

"What?" I say, realizing I shouldn't have said anything.

"Why didn't you fly over here on your broom?" She cackles, exposing more teeth than necessary.

"Watch it or I'll shove it up your ass." I drop the bag of balls and run up the court.

"No, you didn't just say that," she calls after me. When I keep on going she yells, "You'll pay for that."

I can't believe I opened my mouth. Little old me actually got a rise out of Thunder. And I don't even feel bad, because she totally deserved it. I run my hand through my ponytail. I'd much rather be a witch than Thunder any day.

Maybe I don't need Liz as my back-up bitch after all! I decide not to fill her in on my run-in with Thunder yet, because I must complete my mission of total game focus. I practice my shots with Baldwin or a very good stand-in for him. Thunder hisses at me a few times, but I try not to make eye contact with her. I'm not going to let her mess up the game for me.

Coach calls all the Reds over for the usual team huddle. "I want to see good defense out there today. All eyes on the ball."

"Yes, Coach," Maria says, nodding.

"I'm not finished," Coach continues. "Don't let outside forces distract you. You're here to play a game. You can see your friends and family afterwards. For the next hour you are mine." She holds her hands out in front of her and we pile ours on top.

"Go Reds," we all yell, and then pull our hands high into the air.

The starting lineup congregates on the court and the rest of us settle on the bench. I don't even bother looking at the grass or the bleachers. I know no one is waiting for me. Not my dad and not Graham. Liz's mom had to take her sister to the dentist, so even they are not here today.

Today I'm playing for Mom. Wherever she is, I hope she can see me. I picture her sitting on a brightly colored beach towel on the grassy area with her long legs stretched out in front of her, crossed at the ankles. She's wearing a pair of dark sunglasses and slides them down her nose every now and then to get a better glimpse of me. When we make eye contact, she sticks up her pinkie finger. Our secret signal that I'm doing a good job.

The whistle blows and the Reds are at it. The Grays look washed-out on the court.

Coach calls for a time-out and high-fives the starting players. We've got five minutes left in the first quarter and we've already scored six baskets.

She points at me. "Eleven in. Twenty-two out."

I quickly jump up. Did I hear this right—we're up and she wants *moi* on the floor? "Me?"

She nods, like *don't disappoint.*

I'm so glad Thunder is not on the court too. It's hard to keep your eye on the ball when you're worried about someone on your own team growling and flinging insults at you.

It's Gray's ball so I hustle to the far end of the court. Zoey makes a steal and we're back on our side. She's grid-locked and pleads for help with her eyes. I free myself from Number 12 and wave my arms. This time there's no monkey dance.

Zoey glances back and forth, then throws the ball to me. It's mine and I'm ready. I quickly dribble closer to the basket but I can feel Number 12 on my tail. She's quicker than I anticipated. She's in front of me now. But nothing can stop me. I am in control. I can do this. So I dribble forward and then feel like I'm flying. I release the ball midair, but something cuts me off and I fall flat on my face. *Cassia, meet the pavement.*

Everyone is cheering. How cruel. I look up and see that

the ball has made it to the basket. The ref blows the whistle and a bunch of girls rush up to me. Both Reds and Grays.

"Sorry, sorry," Number 12 gasps.

A couple of Red girls try to help me up. But I can't walk. Immense pain radiates from my ankle. Coach steps in, hoists me up, and slings my arm across her shoulder. Then she puts her arm around my waist. "Does it hurt?" she asks.

I just answer with my eyes. This is *so* not happening to me. Two games in a row I screw up. There are no third chances. I'm officially dead.

I hobble off the court, wincing with every step. My focus does not leave the ground. I can't bear to look anyone in the eye.

"I'm so sorry," I whisper to nobody in particular.

Coach has her hand on my shoulder while my leg is stretched out on the bench. "Where do you feel the pain?" she asks.

"Here." I look at my ankle but point to my heart as little droplets run down my face. What if I can't play anymore? Basketball was my best hope yet at finding a passion.

I have to stop crying. This is so stupid, but I can't help it. I wipe my face with the back of my hand. Fingers crossed that people mistake my tears for drops of sweat. "I'm so sorry," I whimper again.

Liz crouches down next to me, removing the hair from my face. "It wasn't your fault."

"Yeah, sure," I say between sniffles. "See, it wasn't meant to be."

"But your hair still looks good," Liz whispers.

The coach from the other team rushes over with a bag of ice and places it on my ankle. The cold feels good.

Maria's mother is standing next to me now, inspecting my ankle. "I'm a nurse. It looks really swollen. She should get it checked out."

Coach Parker leans over me, her whistle swings close to my nose. "Can you reach your folks?"

Before I have a chance to answer, Liz says, "I'll call my mom. She'll take her."

"No, I'm here." I feel a strong hand on my shoulder. I look up. It's Lucien. "It's okay, kiddo," he whispers into my ear.

black twizzlers

There's nothing glamorous about sitting in the washed-out waiting room of Simmons Hospital. The last time I was here was when I was nine and had a really bad sore throat. I was up half the night coughing and Dad rushed me over without even calling my pediatrician. It turned out I had bronchitis.

It's hard to think that if maybe Mom had made it to this gloomy place, she might have lived. She died in the ambulance on the way to the hospital. It's less than a five-minute ride from our condo.

I was in school that day and went home with my teacher, Mrs. Morgan. Dad didn't pick me up until after dark. He looked very old and tired when he came to Mrs. Morgan's front door. His eyes were red and puffy. When he kneeled down to pick me up, I kissed his cheek. It tasted salty like French fries.

That night when he tucked me in bed, he told me that Mom was with the angels and was watching over me. I stared at the ceiling long after he left my room, hoping to catch a glimpse of her. All I wanted was to see her wings flutter.

———

When Lucien and I are finally settled in the decaying red plastic chairs that are nailed to the ground, I ask him, "How come you were at my game?"

"Because I wanted to see you play." He smiles.

"Thanks! But why is it that you can surprise me while Dad obviously can't."

"Actually, your father wanted to come, but he needed to finish the painting for the opening of the new wing at Clement House tonight. You can't have a brand-new section added to a home for children without a painting of the place."

"I guess not," I sigh. If only I had decided to spend the summer watching Dad paint, like last summer, then I wouldn't be here in pain. Oh yeah, I'd probably be in a different kind of pain, though, watching some chick drool all over him. Don't know which is worse at this point.

"I know your dad isn't always there when you need him, but he loves you very much. Trust me." Lucien's blue eyes sparkle and his smile is full. His hair shines under the florescent lights. It's been silver ever since I can remember, and he's never tried to hide it.

"I know, but sometimes I wish…"

A nurse comes out into the waiting area and says, "Cassia Bernard."

I lean against Lucien and hobble into a little room.

The nurse is putting pressure on different parts of my ankle. "Ouch," is all I can mutter.

"You're going to need an x-ray," she says, "to make sure nothing's broken." I run my fingers over my chest again. Did somebody say the same thing to my mom when they found out she had a heart abnormality?

I would never admit this to Lucien, but I wish Dad loved me as much as he loved her.

———

After the x-ray, they put us in an even narrower room with a TV. I imagine this is what jail is like, minus the tube, of course. It's a cell-free zone, so Lucien steps out to give my dad an update. I lie down on the bed. My whole body aches, down to the core. If I could disappear into the crisp white bed sheets, I would.

A doctor steps into the room. She's really small, almost like a pixie. "Hello, I'm Dr. Roberts. Are you Cassia?"

I sit up straight. "Yup, that's me."

"Nothing is broken. Just a bad sprain." I peek out into the hall and see what is probably my x-ray up on the light board. It's amazing that a machine can see inside my body. I'm just glad it can't peek inside my soul.

"Do I have to use crutches?" I ask. I've always wanted to try those things. They look cool.

"Yes, but hopefully only for a couple of weeks. Then

give it another few days rest and you should be able to get back on the court." She stares at my red jersey, a dead give-away that I have a team to get back to.

That's if they'll take me back. It'll be the end of the session and I'm sure everyone will have forgotten me by then.

Lucien pops back into the room and shakes hands with Dr. Roberts. "Are you Cassia's father?" Dr. Roberts asks.

"Her uncle." Lucien smiles.

She repeats the same info about my ankle and says a nurse will be in with my crutches while she prepares my discharge papers.

"Your dad was itching to come to the hospital, but I told him we're almost done and I'd bring you over to the gallery." Lucien takes a packet of Lifesavers out of his shirt pocket and offers me one.

I pull a red one from the pack. Then I look down at my ankle.

"Don't worry. I'll drop you up front," he says.

———

These crutches are definitely going to take some getting used to. It's less than ten feet from the car to the door and my armpits already ache.

"Hello, Cassia. Are you all right?" Monica runs up and gives me a big hug.

"Yeah, I'm fine. Just sore."

She pulls up a chair for me and a second one for my

foot. "Stay here. I'll get your father. He was really worried about you."

I doubt it.

Dad comes running down the stairs. He's wearing an old T-shirt and it's covered with vermilion paint. Red, no longer the color of victory. Now the color of the wounded.

"*Ma cherie*, I feel terrible. How are you? I wanted to come, but Lucien told me to stay and finish…"

"It's okay, Dad. I'm fine. Only a sprain. But it looks like my career in basketball is over." Followed by my life. Finding passion, take one: Total Fail.

"Oh, no, don't say that." He leans down next me. "A few weeks rest and you'll be as good as new."

"Maybe. But now I have to limp around on these things." I point to the crutches.

Dad picks them up and hobbles across the room.

"Not bad, Dad."

"Broke my foot once skiing. Was on these babies for a full month."

"You used to ski?"

"I dabbled." He laughs.

His cell rings and he leans on one crutch to answer it. "Hi, Helga. Can't talk right now, but Cassia's fine. Just a bad sprain. Call you later." He quickly ends the call.

If my ankle was broken, would he have taken her call?

"So where were we?" Dad hands my crutches back.

"Nowhere." I glare at him.

"Oh, I know what I wanted to tell you." He taps my shoulder.

What, that Helga broke her ankle once too?

"Yeah?" I roll my eyes.

"So, you don't want to know about Graham, then?" Dad stands in front of me with his hand on his hip like he's dangling a carrot above my head.

"What about him?" I jump for the carrot.

"He called and I told him what happened. He's coming by to see you. Should be here any minute."

He wants to see me? I'm covered with freeze-dried sweat. That's what I call the Florida effect. You sweat like a pig, go into the a/c, then your sweat is freeze-dried against your body. I look down at my fat ankle. Not the prettiest sight.

"You should really try to get to know Graham. He's a nice kid." Dad pulls a cigarette from behind his ear and heads out the back door.

Pshaw! If he only knew it's been my secret plan all along. Actually, I want more than to get to know Graham. I want to recreate little Graham crackers with him.

I'm too tired to even bother inching to the bathroom to freshen up. The only thing I do is pull the elastic from my ponytail and brush my hair out. I scan the room and notice that something is wrong. Terribly wrong.

Lady in Red is not in her usual spot. I look around to see if she was moved, perhaps to a more central location. But no. She's not anywhere. How could Dad sell her without me knowing? I didn't even get to say goodbye. I've told him many times how much I love that painting. How could he forget?

"Is this the patient?" Graham's standing in front of me, holding an electric-pink sketchbook.

"Afraid so."

He looks down at my swollen ankle wrapped in an ace bandage. "I know you'll be back on the court soon, but I got this for you in case you get bored." He hands me the sketchbook.

I open it up. The fresh white pages make a crinkly sound when I turn them. No guy has ever given me a present before. I take a quick whiff; it even smells like him. Vanilla Rain.

"Thanks, that was really nice of you." I look down at my foot. "It even matches my ankle."

Graham pulls up a chair and straddles it so he's facing me. "Great. I always try to color coordinate."

Then why's he wearing a burnt-umber shirt and shorts? Unless he's auditioning for a role as a UPS guy, it's a definite no.

Graham has the arm with the scar on top of the chair, but quickly puts it down. I guess he's self-conscious about something. Well, that makes two of us.

"So how's it going with my dad?" I ask.

"Great. He knows so much. I'm learning tons about depth and texture."

Still the superhero. "Yeah, he's a good teacher." I pull my hair all to one side.

Graham sits up straight and gives me the once-over. "You did something to your hair. It looks real shiny."

What is it with these artists? It takes them forever to notice a big change. "Yeah, I dyed it last night. Just wanted to do something different. Liz calls me Licorice Chick."

Okay, that ranks high on the dweeb-o-meter.

"Twizzlers?" Graham asks.

"Huh?" Is he serious? "Twizzlers are red."

"But don't they come in other colors too?" He smiles. "Anyway, they look good on you."

He likes my hair? Oh my God, all is not lost. Graham Hadley likes *my* hair!

jagged tawny rocks

It's been five days since I sprained my ankle, and I'm officially bored. Coach left a message on my voicemail on Friday asking how I was feeling. She also said to go down to the Y today and sign up for another class until I'm cleared to play ball again. I could just take the time off and chill, but it's not like I can hang out at the beach or cruise the mall with my crutches. Instead, I'd be glued to the sofa watching soaps or overcrowding Dad and Graham at the studio. Not that I don't want to be around Graham 24/7, but I'm taking Liz's approach and trying to play it cool.

The most annoying thing about having a sprained ankle is actually getting around. My condo is not a big deal, since we have an elevator and it's only three steps down from the lobby to the front entrance, but it's a good ten-minute walk to the Y. Luckily, there's a bus stop on the corner of my street, so that's where I'm sitting now.

The Number 10 pulls up and I crutch aboard. I sit right up front in the handicapped section. The bus drops me off and I go straight to the camp director's office, like Coach Parker instructed me to. I hope to have some say in what class they stick me in, but as long as it doesn't involve any physical activity, I'll be fine.

"Hi, I'm Cassia Bernard and I'm supposed to change my class since I can't play basketball right now," I tell the lady in the burgundy dress sitting at the big metal desk. She looks like a vintage wine that's been tucked away in the cellar for years. I look around the room for a window and spot one behind a huge stack of books. This place could really use a little sunshine.

She peers up from a pile of papers. "Yes, Mrs. Parker told me you were going to come by." Burgundy lady pulls a piece of paper out of a drawer. "Take a look at the classes we offer. A few are full, but let me know what you're interested in."

I scan the list. Volleyball. Out. Swimming. Out. Drama. Still involves a lot of movement. Painting and drawing. I might as well join Dad and Graham. My injury really limits my find-a-passion quest. I turn the page. I don't want to be forced into something like computer design or cosmetology. There's no space to record likes and dislikes on my college applications, so I might as well find something I can stick to.

My eyes stop on ceramics. This could work. It's something I've always wanted to try and if I like it, then I can definitely change my fall school schedule. I know you have to work the wheel, but that only involves one foot and my right foot is fine.

"How about ceramics?" I ask.

The lady pulls out another list. This one is pages long. She flips through a few. "Yes, I believe Mr. Parker has a couple of open slots."

"Mr. Parker?" As in, the husband to my basketball coach, the lady I was sure got cozy with her ball at night? "Any relation to Ms. Parker, the basketball coach?"

"Yes, *Mrs.* Parker is married to *Mr.* Parker." She gets up from the desk and walks toward the door like this is not shocking news. "Follow me. I'll introduce you to him."

Okay, this is getting weirder. Not only did I picture Mrs. Parker as Ms. Parker, living alone, but if she's married, it would not be to a ceramics teacher but to a college football coach.

The art room is down the hall. Mr. Parker is seated at his desk, tapping away on his computer. Burgundy lady points to me and asks, "Eli, do you have room for one more?"

He looks up, laughing, and turns the computer monitor to face us. His cheeks are rosy and he has a wild beard. Neanderthal meets Bill Gates. Totally not Ms. Parker-esque. His hair is as wild as hers is perfect.

"I did it!" he bellows. We're staring at his face on the body of a sumo wrestler. Weird.

Burgundy laughs, so I do too, just to be polite.

"Sure, I have room," Mr. Parker says. "What's your name?"

"Cassia Bernard."

He strokes his beard and stares at me. "What a pretty name. Cassia, as in *Cassia fistula*?"

Only a serious plant lover would pick up on that. Most people think I'm named after the constellation Cassiopeia. "Yup, the golden shower plant."

"Well, pleasure to have you, Cassia. Call me Eli. All the other students do. There's an empty seat at the first table. Class starts in fifteen minutes."

I lean against my crutches. "I thought I was going to sign up and come back tomorrow. I'm not even prepared."

"All you need are these." He shakes his hands in the air like a belly dancer.

It's not like I have anything else to do, so I place my crutches against the wall and take a seat on the stool. This room is set up pretty much like a school art room. Teacher's desk up front, four worn-out wooden art tables with stools, four potter's wheels, and an oversized metal cabinet for supplies.

Since they're more than three weeks into the session, Mr. Parker (I mean Eli) said I have some catching up to do, but I'm welcome to stay after if I like. He definitely knows how to make someone feel welcome.

A few kids trickle in. Nobody I know; all around my age, though. A boy in a yellow Charlie Brown shirt sits down next to me. He's got black-rimmed glasses on and his chin pierced, and he seems nice enough. There's one other girl at my table. Her hair is black too, but cropped really short.

Eli gives me a quick introduction. Everyone says hi. Then he grabs a hunk of terra-cotta clay and slaps it down in front of me. "Don't be afraid to really get to know the clay. You own it." God, he sounds just like his wife. *Get to know the ball.* "The first project is done by hand. After that you'll learn to work the wheel," he tells me.

Then he hands out people's fired projects and talks to them for a couple of minutes about the glazing process. He says you have to apply several coats, then wait for one to dry before applying the next or the color will end up uneven—dark in some spots, light in others. Sounds like the painting I hung in my bedroom window in fifth grade. I painted a multi-colored butterfly and faced it to the street so that it could look out at the people below and wouldn't be lonely. When I took it down a year later, the blue construction paper it was mounted on was completely faded in the front, but the back remained a deep ocean blue. The butterfly, however, held on strong and was still bright and cheery.

I stare at the blob of clay. It looks like an unborn baby ready to be formed. I don't want to be the one to ruin it for life. I glance around the room. Nobody seems to be in limbo; they're all busy, lost in their projects. My pointer finger slides into the clay. It's cool and moist. I close my eyes and mash it with my palm. It feels smooth, much different from the pimply touch of the basketball skin. After the clay has softened, I roll it into a ball.

The girl next to me is using Rockin' Red glaze on her

coffee mug and the boy on the other side of me is painting his cappuccino cup chartreuse. I wish I could skip right to the color. It really adds a lot of personality to their pieces. It looks like their assignment was to make something to drink out of. I could ask Eli if I should start with that, but he's way too into picture-morphing on his computer right now. The coffee mug seems easiest, so I flatten my ball and start molding.

Everyone is pretty quiet. Eli has a CD on, playing classical music, and only a couple of girls at the last table are chatting. This place is so much mellower than the basketball court. It's like you're on your own here. Everyone speaks in hushed tones, but I'm half expecting them to yell, "I'm open" or "Pass over here." No, they're more like, "Dude, can I use your small brush?" No one's in a hurry; it's such a different environment. You'd think I've been playing basketball all my life, not just three weeks.

Eli comes over and shows me how to smooth the inside of my mug so that it doesn't crack in the kiln. "If you have any questions, you can ask Nia." He points to the girl sitting at my table.

She looks up from her mug and gives me a little wave.

"Hi," I say back. "Have you been doing this a long time?"

"I took ceramics when I went to sleepaway camp two summers ago."

The kid with the piercing chimes in. "Nia's good at everything."

"Not true, Scott," she says. Her voice is small but powerful.

"Oh, sorry. Except for calling people back." He has a smirk on his face. His mini-smile reminds me of Graham. Who am I kidding? The fact that he's from the male species remind me of Graham. Graham's probably so busy inhaling my father's paint fumes right now that he doesn't even notice I'm not there.

"You know I lost my cell," Nia whines.

Scott's face turns red.

Clearly, this is something personal. Subject change. Quick. "Is there any trick to making the handle?" I hold a piece of clay up that looks like a snake.

"Shorten it first. Then you need to slip and score," Nia says.

I coil the handle around my finger. "What's that?" All I picture is someone trying to score a basket and slipping on a banana peel. I don't mention this to Nia. Last thing I need is a light-up sign over my head flashing the word *amateur*.

She hands me a knife. "Scratch lines on your mug where you're going to attach the handle." She watches me make the scratch marks and hands me some watery clay— "the slip." I affix it to the mug. Then she instructs me to press the handle onto the mug.

"Good. Just keep some pressure on it." Nia gets up from the table and walks over to the sink.

"Women." Scott shakes his head like I understand what he's going through.

"Definitely," I answer and stretch out my leg.

Scott gestures to my foot. "How'd you do that?"

"Playing basketball."

"You play ball? That's cool."

Do I *not* look like a ball player? What do I look like? "Cool until this sprain."

"I sprained my ankle too, once. Boy Scout camping trip. We were on a hike."

I look up at the silver stud in his chin and his bed-head. He *so* does not look like a Boy Scout. "Yeah, it seems like everyone has a crutches story. Even my dad."

"Everyone except Nia." Scott laughs. "She probably walked at three months old."

———

I spend the rest of the class "getting to know the clay." I start with basic shapes, then move on to a butterfly. It's like I'm back in preschool molding my red Play-doh. The only difference is, Gabe Wilde isn't here to eat the leftover pieces off of the plastic table.

I pass the shelf of glazes on the way out. I run my finger over the bottles on the top. Celadon. White Crackle. Temmoku. If I did stay after it would be to add some color to my mug. Too bad I have to wait for it to be fired. Maybe I'll paint it white. It's such a pure color; it hides nothing.

"Thanks, Eli. That was a lot of fun," I say as I pass his desk.

He's cropping a picture of a dog on the computer. Looks like a golden retriever. Don't tell me he wants to be a dog now. "Glad you enjoyed it, Cassia. Stick with it and you'll see that you can create marvelous things with your hands."

I make my way awkwardly through the door and outside the building. The pads of the crutches are digging into my underarms. I tighten the straps on my backpack, then rest against the brick wall and wait for the bus. I think about what Mr. Parker said about my hands, whether he says it to every student.

My cell vibrates in my pocket. It's Liz. "Hey, girl, what's up?" I say.

"Harry and I are officially a couple now." I can tell she's still in the middle of her happy dance.

"That's awesome. But I thought you already were. What did he say?"

"We met for lunch and he said he wanted us to be exclusive."

Funny. Graham and I met at the gallery and now he's exclusive with my dad. I know it's not the same thing, but still… "That's so cool." I try to sound excited.

The bus pulls up to my stop and lets out a huge sigh.

"Where are you?" Liz asks.

I slide closer to the bus, cell phone tucked between my ear and shoulder, waiting for everyone to get off. A few droplets of water settle on my head. Rain and crutches, not a good combination. I can't risk spraining my good ankle. "I'm at the Y, I decided to…"

"Oh my God," Liz shouts. "I forgot to tell you the best part."

"Okay, what?" My arms already ache and I haven't even walked a half a block.

"Harry bought me the cutest teddy bear. He said his name is Hariz. Get it!" She laughs.

No.

I can't talk, get on a bus, and crutch at the same time. The rain is getting heavier. "Liz, I'm getting all wet. I'll call you later," I say, and hang up.

I ride the sweaty bus in silence. I guess the a/c is out, unless it's the bus driver's evil intention to suffocate us. He has a mini-fan up front cooling the driver's seat.

I open the new sketchbook that Graham gave me and take a whiff to see if it still smells like him. I come up with nothing. I grab a pencil out of my bag so that no one thinks I'm a crazy book sniffer. Except for Graham's behind, I haven't drawn in a while, but Mr. Parker's class jump-started the creative side of my brain.

The pencil leads the way. I start with a few zigzags on top of the page and move to an oval. Then I draw a pair of eyes. Deep eyes. I center them a thumbnail apart from each other and quickly sketch the nose. It's long and pointy. I draw past the 64th Street stop, past the 68th Street stop. I don't look up. I just hear the bus screech to a halt and take off again. The rain pounds against the windows. It's only summer rain, so I know it'll end soon. Next we zoom past my stop. No one gets on or off. Not even me. I can't stop drawing. Not now. I'm revved up like a race-car engine. I can't remember when I last had so many emotions running through me. It feels good to be alive.

A few minutes later, I glance up from my paper. The rain has let up. The sun is bright like nothing ever happened; only scattered drops roll down the window. The next stop is Sunny Isles, blocks from my house. I get off and cross the street. Thankfully there's a bench to sit on and wait for a bus back to Miami Beach. I'm still clutching my sketchbook. I open it and trace my fingers over the finished product.

An old man sits down next to me. He rests his cane between us. "Are you an artist?" he asks.

I look down at the picture. It's Thunder, and the tip of a lightning bolt is striking her enormous head. I don't know if this is art. "I try," I answer.

"I used to draw." The old man's eyes are pale blue like the sky.

"Me too," I whisper.

Then I glance back down at Thunder's face. If you look past the dark circles under her eyes, all you see is sadness. Her eyes are like jagged tawny rocks at the bottom of the ocean. I'm glad I don't have a mirror to peer inside my own eyes.

black and white

It's funny how one minute you're in and the next minute you're out. Okay, I was just coming back from the dead after my screw-up against the Brown team, but I thought that the game against Gray was going to be my comeback. My victory was short-lived, of course. I look down at my ankle. The swelling is way down, but it still hurts when I put pressure on it.

So here I am, watching the team I was a part of a mere week ago, and now I feel like an outsider. Sure, everyone came over before the game started and asked how I felt, but when the whistle blew, they were gone. I don't even feel like I'm supposed to be here. On the bench. If it weren't for Liz, I probably wouldn't have come. I don't really see the point of hanging around like an invalid groupie. It makes me feel even more alone.

I try to focus on the game, feel something for my

team. The Reds hustle, pass, and shoot. A Green steals the ball, but Liz quickly snatches it back. I spot a stray ball under the bench and pick it up. I twirl it around in my hands. There's something so natural feeling about the circular motion. Maybe in my past life I was a basketball player (wonder if they had basketball back then), and so I'm drawn to it. Either that or I was a microwave, defrosting one frozen entrée at a time.

It could be that we're born with a passion, but that the desire lays dormant until it's awakened. Perhaps when you come in contact with your destined passion a few times, your body fuses the connection. But if that were the case then I'd have already known that basketball was my passion, because I've played enough pickup games over the years. Maybe my passion is something close to the word basketball, but my brain sent a misfire. Like basket weaving! I'm not sure how I feel about that. I do like crafts, but one can only have so many baskets.

Harry is sitting with Liz's family. He's cheering Liz on, even giving her a standing ovation every time she makes a good play. Graham hardly noticed my new hair color, and Harry notices every time Liz makes a decent pass. Heck, they even have a teddy bear named after their perfect union. Maybe I have my eyes on the wrong guy, but even so, there's something that really draws me to Graham. He has the Prince Charming gene and he's smart to boot.

I should stop by the gallery more often. If anything, I could use a little stare at his butt to cheer myself up. Dad's come home late these past few nights. I know he's been with the touchy-feely Helga lady because he strolls in the door whistling. I pretend to be asleep when he passes my bedroom. I don't want to see the smile or the smudge of lipstick she left on his face.

The Reds win against the Greens, 49 to 22. Confidence tramples self-respect. The chili peppers out-spice the green beans. Green was the last of the five teams— now we start again and play each team one more time. We've won three out of the five games so far; not bad. If we win a few more we could move on to the finals. The finals take place over a couple of days, winner takes home the trophy.

"Hey, crip, we won without you today." Thunder smiles at me, sweat dripping from her forehead. I never noticed her mustache before. Looks like it's time for a shave.

I don't say anything, but as she starts to walk away, I extend one of my crutches. She lets out a yelp but catches herself before she falls. "Bitch," she growls.

I just smile. I'm learning that a little dig goes a along way. The trick is to stay calm, even if you're fuming inside.

Liz's family is nearby. I stand up and hobble across the court to find them. Coach Parker stops me midway. "How is everything?"

"Fine. Foot's doing a lot better."

Zoey walks past us and smiles, the sympathy kind, not the I'm-so-happy-to-see-you kind.

"Good. We're hoping you'll be able to return before season's over."

"You want a screw-up back?" I ask, half joking, half not.

Coach's eyes widen and her face goes all serious. "Cassia, what made you ever think that?"

"It's just that I messed up an important play, and now this." I peer down at my ankle. "It's almost like payback."

"No, I don't want you to ever think that. It's all part of the game. Winning, losing, and unfortunately injuries do happen. What seems huge to you, others have already forgotten about."

"I guess you're right." I look out at the team scattered around, talking and laughing. But Thunder is just standing there with her arms crossed. She's probably not forgotten. "I do tend to overreact sometimes." I stretch my ankle out but quickly wince from the pain.

"We all do, but don't be so hard on yourself, okay?" Coach smiles.

"I'll try." I throw her a smile back.

"Let me know if you need anything, all right?" She pats me on the shoulder.

I hope I don't look like a lost soul. A lone flower blowing in the wind.

I thank Coach, then get up and hobble past Thunder and her boyfriend. He has his arm firmly around her neck. I shudder. The mere size of him gives me the creeps. They make a good couple. They're both scowling. They would not cut it in ceramics. No one in that class is vying for the title *Bully of the Year*. They leave you alone, and even if there's something going on, like between Scott and Nia, it's all fun.

Liz's mom offers me a ride home. This time I take it. I ride in front, so I can stretch my leg out. Liz is sandwiched in the back of the Jeep Liberty with Harry and her little sister, Crystal.

"So how's Graham?" Harry asks.

I turn to face him. "Fine, I guess. Haven't seen him in a couple of days."

"He seems like a cool dude." Harry rolls the window down halfway even though the a/c is on full blast.

Liz leans forward, resting her elbow on the back of my seat. "Cass has a plan. She's going to *wow* him with her beauty and intellect."

Harry laughs.

"Thanks," I mutter under my breath.

"Kidding." Harry reaches over Crystal and taps my shoulder.

I think Crystal is light-years ahead of the rest of the fourth grade population because she immediately changes the subject and fills us in on every detail of her day at soccer camp. I've never been so happy to learn how to head-butt a ball. It would be a definite no-no in basketball, though. I really don't need a brain injury.

"Cassia, what are you doing now that you can't play basketball?" Mrs. Betancourt asks me.

"I'm taking a ceramics class at the Y."

"You are?" Liz asks.

I turn around again. "I tried to tell you the other day, but you were kind of spacey."

"When?" Liz furrows her brows. I know she's insulted, but it's the truth.

"You called me on the cell to tell me *stuff*."

"Oh, yeah." A little smirk spreads across her face. "Well, tell us about the class."

"It's pretty chill so far. Really laid back. And the funniest thing is, the teacher is Coach Parker's husband."

"No way!" Liz shrieks. "What's he like? I totally thought she was gay."

"Me too. He's got hair the color of cinnamon toast, and a full beard. Nice guy, let's us do whatever we want."

"My kind of guy," Harry chimes in. I don't see Harry as someone who takes direction very well. I think he'd probably be on Coach's shit list if he played ball.

"Does Coach know you're taking a class with her man?" Liz asks.

I shrug. "She didn't mention it and neither did I."

Mrs. Betancourt pulls up to my building. "Thanks for the ride, Mrs. B," I say, trying to wiggle my way out the door without putting too much pressure on my foot.

She gets out of the car and hands me my crutches from the back. "Do you need help getting up the stairs?"

"No, I'm cool, thanks. Bye, guys." I wave to everyone.

I really wish Liz could come over. I know she has plans

with Harry. If I'd asked, she would've said I could tag along. I'm *so* not into being the third wheel. It only makes you realize even more what you don't have. It reminds me of the Mother's Day breakfasts in elementary school. For the first couple of years after Mom died, Dad came instead. All the other mothers stared at us and shot my dad sympathy smiles. After a few years, he stopped coming and said I could stay home if I wanted to. I blocked it out and assumed the role of teacher's helper. I made Mom a card every year and stuck it in a shoebox under my bed. I never put the lid on the box, just in case she wanted to take a peek at her cards. But I was glad when I went to middle school and the Mother's Day festivities stopped.

I'm totally exhausted after I get inside my condo. For one thing, my armpits are killing me. I'm surprised they're not bleeding. Nobody told me there was going to be arm pain involved with spraining your ankle. I'll be so glad when I get rid of these crutches next week.

I let my crutches fall to the floor and I half hop, half lean against the wall and furniture to make my way to the couch. I grab a blanket and turn on the TV, my only dependable friend.

Besides getting up to go to the bathroom and grabbing a granola bar, I spend the afternoon on the couch. Being a couch potato has its perks. Although, if my hips start expanding and my chin starts multiplying, I won't be a happy camper.

I make it to five p.m., then shut off the TV. My eyes

droop. It's raining. Not regular summer rain, but tropical-storm-warning rain—the kind where the streets are dark and you have to drive your car at a snail's pace with the lights on if you want to make it home in one piece. It's lulling me to sleep, big time. I bury my head in the couch pillow, but I can still hear the water sloshing against the windows like the washing machine on heavy cycle. I close my eyes. All I see is black.

The man in the black sports car doesn't care about the rain, about the other cars on the road, or even the passenger next to him. The music is pumping full blast. You can't make out the words because the storm and the heavy bass drone out the lyrics. The car screeches to a halt and the passenger is immediately ejected, landing beside a huge oak tree. Her face is masked and in seconds she's soaking from head to toe. Lightning strikes and the car speeds off. The woman has been zapped. Her face is charred black, but she will live.

I shake myself awake. I can't get out of that dream fast enough. I feel like I've been held captive in my own nightmare, but thank God, the girl is not me. It's Thunder. She's invading my personal space now. Yet I can't help but wonder if she's okay. I scoot over to the living room window and see that the sun is shining bright now. It's turned out to be the perfect evening for a walk on the beach, with only a few raindrops still clinging to the window and scattered puddles down below in the parking lot.

Maybe this dream was a wake-up call. My subconscious

could be warning me that Thunder's out for blood. But I figure she'll lay off me while I'm recovering. Even in her twisted head, I don't see how I can be a threat to her when I'm not playing ball. Either way, I need to be on guard for when I return to the court. I just need to be alert and stay one step ahead of her.

Ratting her out to Coach is out of the question because then everyone will think I'm such a wimp. Getting Liz to provoke her is also a no because that will just get Liz thrown off the team and I'd feel terrible about that. Telling Dad would probably backfire and before I know it, Thunder would be seated on my couch licking the wooden spoon from a Hoodsie cup.

Poisoning her water bottle would be a good idea, but let's face it; I don't have much evil in me, even when I try. Causing her to have explosive diarrhea or break out in hives during the game would be more like it. Sending her on a one-way trip to Alaska would work for me, too.

All this thinking is making me hungry. I flip open the cabinet door. Oreo cookies. Black and white. Evil vs. Good. I take out one and screw off the top. I lick off the white icing; the sugar tastes sweet against my tongue. Then I gobble both cookies whole.

ashen tiles

When I crutch through the door of La Reverie a few days later, the first thing I see is the empty spot where *Lady in Red* once sat. It glares at me like a ketchup stain on a white carpet. Can't they fill it up already? At this point I don't even want to know who bought it. I could always peek at Lucien's records, but stalking a painting is a bit much, even for me. Of course, if the info happens to be lying around on his desk…

Looks like Monica is the only one manning the shop. "Do you know where my dad is?" I ask.

She glances at her watch. "It's noon already? Wow! He said he'd be back around now. He gave a talk at the museum this morning about his flower exhibit."

"Okay." I inch my way back behind Lucien's desk. "What about Lucien?"

"He's on his way out. His niece and nephew are in town today. He's meeting them for lunch."

Speaking of lunch, I'm pretty hungry. I hope there are some Saltines waiting for me in the desk drawer.

"That's cool," I say. "So how's your nephew?"

"Thomas is good, thanks. He's in New York right now visiting some of his cousins."

"Cool. He's lucky." *This is pathetic. I'm jealous of someone I hardly know, and who knows if he's even having fun in the Big Apple.*

Monica adjusts *Moon Bisque* on the wall. "Everything okay, Cassia?"

Yes! A whole sleeve of crackers, unopened. "Yeah, I'm cool. Just trying to deal with being partially immobile."

"I sprained my ankle once, too. Fell down a flight of stairs. Was a real bummer."

"Bummer, you can say that again." *You and everyone else. What do you have to do to be special around here? Be in a full-body cast?*

Lucien comes charging down the stairs from the studio. I have a whole cracker stuffed in my mouth. "Hi," I mumble.

"Hey, kiddo." He rushes over and gives me a huge hug. "Angie and Dave are in town today. Want to join us for a bite?"

He only gets to see them a couple of times a year but sees me practically every day. "No, thanks. I've got my lunch right here." I pat the packet of Saltines.

"Waiting around for someone special?" Lucien raises an eyebrow.

"Monica said Dad should be back any minute."

"That's not who I meant." Lucien punches me in the shoulder and lets out a laugh.

"Well, if Graham happens to stop by, that'd be fine with me." I blush.

"Hang onto him, kiddo. He's a great guy."

"Trust me, if I can, I will."

The door chimes and Monica scurries to the front.

"Speak of the devil," Lucien says, a little too loudly, and escapes out the back door. The devil is really the only thing that gives red a bad rap. Graham is dressed in a purple shirt. What does that make him? Barney?

I wave to the guy in purple and he walks toward me. So much for me snooping in Lucien's desk and learning the whereabouts of *Lady in Red*.

"How are you feeling?" Graham asks, portfolio in hand, of course.

"Fine, thanks."

"Good. Is your dad here?"

Already done with me?

"No, he'll be back soon, though." I fold the top of the cracker packet and shove them back in the drawer. I don't need a replay of our first meeting.

"Mind if I hang?" He leans against the desk.

Mind? Ha, if he only knew. "No, grab a chair." I point to an empty seat against the wall.

Graham tugs on the back of his shirt and sits down. Why is he wearing the color usually reserved for eggplants? It's not my favorite color for a guy, but if anyone can pull it off, he can. Purple is the color of energy. They should've made the Energizer Bunny purple. Maybe Graham's here to re-energize me. I could plug myself in and bing, I'd feel better.

"Thanks." He pulls up next to me and swipes a rubber band off the desk.

"I'd love to see your work. I never really got a chance when you brought your portfolio by before." *I was too busy staring at your butt.*

"Sure." He looks around the gallery. "Do you think you could make it up the stairs? I could display them on the easels."

I stand up, putting all my weight on my good foot. This is not very comfortable. "Yeah, that sounds good," I say. Why do I feel like one of those sleazy frat-party guys who eases the girl up to his bedroom, then draws the shades and jumps her bones? But as much as I would like to jump Graham's bones, I don't want to do it in my dad's studio. Never mind that I'm a total chickenshit.

Graham carries my crutches up the stairs, along with his portfolio case, while I hobble up, holding on to the railing. I feel like a dork hopping up the stairs, my boobs jumping up and down and my ponytail flopping from side to side. *Graham, is this the girl you want to date? I think not!*

When we get into the studio Graham displays the pieces on a few empty easels. I turn the radio dial until I pick up some slow jams. I hate dead air. Graham sets up two folding chairs in front of the exhibit.

"The show is now up and running." He motions me over.

I take a seat and eye the other empty one.

"You need to keep your foot elevated. Besides, the artist never sits," Graham says, hands in his pockets just deep enough to cover most of the scar on his left arm. I wonder if he stuck his hands in the pockets before he bought the shorts, or if he could tell just by looking at them that they had deep enough pockets to hide his only imperfection.

"He doesn't?" I'm not sure if he's kidding about the artist not sitting or if this is something I should take note of.

"Shall we?" He points to the first piece.

"Mmm." I nod at the abstract.

"*Chameleon Exposed.*"

It's a wild swirl of colors wrapped around the trunk of a tree. It's almost blinding. I look away but am immediately drawn back to it. There's something so pure about this painting. He didn't follow any rule of color, swirling neutrals, bolds, and lukewarms together, but somehow it works. That's what I like about art. Even though there are rules, they're meant to be broken and if you do it right, you're hailed a genius. I guess kind of like my dad. It's funny how you can be so good at one thing and crappy at everything else. Well, my dad's not crappy at everything, but he lacks simple skills like paying bills on time, making pancakes that don't burn, and showing up for appointments. It's like all his brain power is sucked up by the need to create.

Graham has moved on to the next painting. "I call this one *Determination*." It's a painting of a super-skinny palm tree surrounded by other palm trees that have fallen to the ground. The interesting thing is, it's only in two colors—pea green and mossy brown.

"Wow, that's cool." I scoot my chair a little closer. "Sad, too. Even the choice of colors."

Graham bites his lip. "It's the will to survive."

"Do you think we're all born with it?"

Graham pulls at a loose screw on the easel. "Yeah, I think we all have it, but not everyone finds it in time."

I think of Mom the last few weeks before she died. She was always pretty thin, but I remember how her clothes hung shapelessly off her body. I don't think she was eating much and her face was as pale as our ashen bedroom tiles. Of course, I didn't know she was dying then, but even at five, I sensed something was wrong. Very wrong.

Graham rests his hand on my shoulder. "Are you all right?"

"Me?" I look up into his eyes. Deep green. If they were a body of water, there would be no depth. What is he thinking? That I'm crazy?

I shake off the image of Mom curled up on the couch in sweats. "Yeah, do you think people have a better chance of living if they really want to?" I ask.

We both stare at the small tree. What makes it stronger than the rest? I rub my fingers over my sprained ankle. "Did you paint it because you lost someone?"

Graham stands awkwardly, one foot in front of the other. His shoulders are hunched. He pulls his hands in and out of his pockets. The scar appearing, then quickly disappearing, pink like a worm. "You mean, like death?"

"Yes." I feel both nervous and excited that we're entering uncharted waters, but with Graham everything rolls off my tongue easily.

He looks down at his sneaks. Green and white Adidas. "Well, sort of. My grandfather died when I was ten. He was a real strong guy, but he had cancer. Fought it until the end."

"I'm so sorry," I say instinctively, because those are the words I heard over and over again after Mom's death. The words I blocked out after hearing them for the thousandth time. "What about your parents?" I ask.

He stretches his legs out in front of him. His surfer's tan glows under the neon studio lights. "What do you want to know?"

"What are they like?"

"Cool for the most part. My dad lives in Fort Lauderdale and I live with my mom and stepdad. I also have a younger brother, Kevin. He's three. A wild dude, too."

I picture a mini-Graham running around in Superman PJs screaming *cowabunga!* "What do they think about your paintings?"

"My dad doesn't say much. He owns a construction company and wants me to go into business with him after college. Mom and my stepdad, Darren, try to understand my work. I think my biggest fan is Kevin. He calls this one Spiderman's house." Graham points to a black-and-white abstract that looks like an intricately woven web.

"Kevin sounds like a smart kid."

"He's got a good role model." Graham laughs.

"Yeah, sometimes I wish I had a brother or sister," I say.

Graham pulls up a chair and sets it down beside me. "What about you?"

"What about me?" I pull at a button on the pocket of my shorts.

Graham's face tightens and his voice softens. "I remember reading something about your mom's death. Are you okay?"

A small lump forms in the back of my throat. I try and gulp it away. I will not cry. Not now. I haven't cried over Mom in years and I'm not about to do it in front of Graham. *Think happy thoughts.* The Miami sunset. Chocolate chip ice cream. Graham. I let go of the words before I change my mind. "My mother died when I was five of a heart abnormality." There, I said it.

"Wow." He takes my hand in his. "Man, that must've been hard."

"My dad and I. We managed." Suddenly it dawns on me that I'm inches away from Graham's face, from holding him tight. I stare up at him. At his full cinnamon lips. I think about how scrumptious they would taste. I imagine his kiss to be sweet and moist.

"Still it must have been hard because you were so young.

I mean, I felt like crap when my parents got divorced. I was nine." He gives my hand a squeeze. A bolt of lightning revs up my heart.

"Yeah, but I have a lot of memories. And lots of questions about her, too. It's almost her birthday." I gulp the lump in my throat away again. "I'm always going through the old albums. She was beautiful."

"I bet." Graham nods, sincerely, then leans closer to me. My heart beats faster than a steel drum. Is he going to kiss me? Yeah, right. I can keep on dreaming. Instead, he pulls me out of my seat and my heart slows to the beat of a bass drum. "Come here. I want to show you something I found when I was looking for some paintbrushes the other day."

I lean against him and hobble over to the supply closet. His body is solid, like I imagine a superhero's to be. It sends warm currents through me. I hope he can't tell I'm shaking inside.

He digs through a few canvases. Pulls one out and dusts it off with his hand. The bodies of the two people are fully formed, but their faces have no features. I feel like I'm losing my footing. Graham grips me tightly at the waist. A tear trickles down my face and into my open mouth. It tastes salty like the ocean.

The figures. They both have long hair, one a shade darker than the other, and they're both dressed in red. The smaller dress is a replica of the larger. It still hangs in the back of my closet. Mom and I standing faceless on the balcony of my condo.

melted mocha ice cream

I wipe my tears and catch my breath just in time to hear Dad's footsteps on the stairs. I know it's him because he makes a clomping sound when he walks. When I was little he said it was because one of his legs was wooden. I believed him until I pinched it so hard that he screamed, "Mercy!"

"Quick, put it away." I elbow Graham. He shoves the painting back in the closet.

"Hi, *ma cherie*. Graham." Dad nods. "Sorry I'm late. Lost track of time." He smells like smoke. He's running late, but had time to light up. I look at the clock on my cell—1:21. If Dad had a nine-to-five job, he would've been canned a long time ago.

"No problem." Graham starts putting his canvases back into his portfolio case. Wouldn't it be nice for once if Dad showed up on time? Why is he so selfish?

Dad runs over to his desk and rummages through the drawers, no doubt looking for a misplaced item. I plunk back down on the folding chair. Suddenly my foot is throbbing from the pressure. Dad's back is to me. His hair is wild, crying out for a haircut.

"Who bought *Lady in Red*?" I blurt out.

Dad doesn't answer me. He's still fumbling around at his desk.

"I said, who bought *Lady in Red*? Was it that woman?" I picture her warming my dad up with a bottle of wine, then whispering in his ear that she'd like nothing more than to see the painting rest above her four-poster bed.

Dad drops a pile of papers and finally turns around to face me. "What woman?"

"You know who I'm talking about, Dad. Your girlfriend."

"You mean Helga?" His eyebrows cling together.

"*Hell-ga* bought *my* favorite painting?"

"Cassia, what has gotten into you? Helga's a very nice woman. She's always asking about you."

I tap my foot. "You didn't answer my question."

"No, she didn't buy the painting."

One of the smaller abstracts slips from Graham's hand. It lands with a thud on his foot. "Ouch." He winces. Only then do I remember he's here. Oh, God, he witnessed my tantrum. I'm *so* stupid.

"Are you okay?" Dad and I ask at the same time.

Graham's face is flushed. "Thanks, I'm fine. Maybe I should leave and come back tomorrow."

"No, I was just leaving. I have plans," I say, and limp over to my crutches resting near the door.

"We'll have dinner tonight. Together." Dad walks over to where Graham is now seated, inspecting the fallen painting but still talking to me. "What do you want to eat?"

"Anything with a face," I say, and shut the door before he asks what I mean. I hobble down the staircase as fast as a wounded person can. I have to get out of this gallery. I need fresh air, and fast. Dad has time to help Graham, but he doesn't have time to paint the faces of me and Mom? How long has that painting been stuffed away in the closet? Probably for years.

"Cassia, is something bothering you?" Dad calls after me, but I've already made it down the stairs.

I don't look at the time until I'm outside. There won't be a bus to the Y for another fifteen minutes. What a pathetic getaway.

———

I'm a mute the first half of ceramics class. I need time to unwind. To forget about Dad, to forget about Graham. Although I'm not too sure I want to forget about Graham. I just hope he'll still talk to me after my mini psycho-girl tirade.

Mr. Parker is standing behind me. It always makes me nervous when teachers do that. "Lighten up, Cassia. Let the clay lead you." The muscles in my shoulders and neck are tense. I let them drop until I feel like a turtle retreating into its shell.

"That's a little better, but I'm not convinced you're relaxed." He laughs. "Why don't we give the wheel a try? But you can't tense up or you'll end up with a square bowl."

I chuckle and follow him to the back of the room, in front of the big window facing an old coconut tree. It's a nice shady spot overlooking the side street. My crutches make funny noises as the rubber bottoms hit the linoleum. Nobody seems to take notice but me. All heads are down, focused on their pieces at different stages of completion.

Mr. Parker hands me an apron, then sits down at the wheel farthest from the window. He tells me to sit down next to him. "I'll give you a mini-tutorial, then let you have a go at it."

"Sure," I say, even though the wheel looks more intimidating than a blank canvas. Really, I'm trying to figure out how the other students created all the elaborate pieces lined up against the windowsill. A pitcher. Two perfectly crafted oversized mugs. A wide-mouthed vase.

Mr. Parker is hunched on the stool in front of the wheel. His back is broad. So maybe he's a former college football player after all. He wets his hands, grabs a ball of clay, and slaps it onto the middle of the wheel. "It's all about centering. If you don't center your piece, it'll be off-kilter and you'll end up fighting the clay the whole time."

I match Mr. Parker's turtlelike posture. I already know how the wheel will feel. Lately I've been totally off balance and it definitely ruins my whole day.

Mr. Parker picks the clay up and throws it down onto

the wheel again. Then he pushes the pedal and the wheel spins. He quickly thrusts the clay into the center. "After you've centered the clay, shape it into a mound. You have to use the force of your whole body to make sure it stays in the middle. When that's done, you're ready to create the opening."

He repeats the process one more time with even more force.

I can't help but giggle. This huge bearded man looks like he's having a wrestling match with a mound of clay.

"Just wait until you get your turn. Sometimes it can take a whole class period to master centering," he says playfully.

I blush. "Oh, I wasn't laughing at you, really. It just seems like the clay is fighting you."

"A rebellion of sorts. I like that." He stops the wheel and flattens what was the beginning of a bowl. "But remember, you're in control. You can't let the clay mold you."

I purse my lips and narrow my eyes. "I'm not afraid."

"Ready to give it a whirl?" He gets up.

I sit in his seat. "Bring it on." I've got nothing to lose.

"Take a deep breath and remember to relax." Mr. Parker steps to the side. "This isn't supposed to be painful."

I stare down at the clay. At the slop of melted mocha ice cream. Dad's favorite flavor at Gianni's on Ocean Drive. Wait, why do I have to share this piece of clay with him? There was a reason I didn't tell him I was coming here. This experience is mine, all mine. That and the fact that he never even asked where I'm going, how I'm spending my basketball-less days. Instead, he's using his brain cells to wine and dine Helga.

Mr. Parker points to the bowl of water next to me. As he instructs, I wet my hands before starting the wheel. I press down on the pedal with my good foot and immediately the clay starts to fly. "Slow down." Mr. Parker holds out his hand like a stop sign.

I start up again but this time much slower. An old Grateful Dead song, "Truckin'," is playing in the background. I guess Mr. Parker and my dad have the same taste in music. I mellow out and start and stop the wheel several times before I'm at a good speed. The song lyrics take me back to when I used to stay up way past my bedtime and watch Dad paint. Whenever I heard the words "doodah man," I burst out laughing. I totally thought they were calling him the doo-doo man. Only funny to a seven-year-old, of course.

Basically that's how I feel, like I'm truckin' along, moving from one project to the next. I don't think there's a sequel to the song, but I'd love to know how the doodah man ended up. Did he find the place he was supposed to be?

My piece of clay is starting to look like a soupy mess, so I ask Mr. Parker if I can exchange it for a new piece. He nods.

I'm back at the wheel, ready for a fresh start. I wet my hands again and throw the clay down. My foot hits the pedal and the clay immediately starts to slide off. I stop the wheel and throw it down again. I put a firm hand on the mound and pray it doesn't start to fly away. Crap, my foot is getting heavy on the pedal and the clay skips a beat. I picture myself sailing across the room to catch it. Luckily, it's not that bad.

This is no joke. I stop and stare at the clay. I can do this. Deep breath, and I'm back at it. My right hand holds the clay down firmer this time. I am in charge.

After several misfires, I actually get my clay centered and flag Mr. Parker down for step two. I'm ready to make an opening. I remember Nia saying last class that it's the trickiest part because you have to keep your hands completely still or you could end up with a lopsided piece before you even get started.

I rest my elbows on my thighs and push the tip of my thumb into the middle of the clay. My hand slips and I have to start over; all part of the learning process, Mr. Parker assures me. I gently push my foot down on the pedal and watch the clay turn circles. I imagine this is what it feels like to drive a car, to brake at a yellow light. I'm signed up for Driver's Ed in the fall—I can't wait to get my license. Not that Dad would even know if I left the city limits. Still, I feel bad that I blew up at him, and even worse that I did it in front of Graham.

But if Dad had just told me where *Lady in Red* was, probably none of this would've happened. I really don't see what the big deal is about who bought it. Maybe the new owner will grant me painting visitation rights.

Scott walks by me to rinse out a mason jar. "Not bad for a first timer. Let me know if you need any help."

"Thanks. I will." I smile. That's so much better than the threats I got from Thunder when I joined the basketball team. There's definitely something up her butt, and I can't figure it out. As mean as she is, her boyfriend looks even meaner. Scary.

Class is over before I even have time to look up at the clock. I thank Mr. Parker on the way out. I had a good day. Being at the wheel was very soothing, and no one cared that I ended up with a bowl that couldn't hold more than a couple spoonfuls of soup.

I check my cell while I wait for the bus. Two new messages. I kind of hope one is from Dad, but both are from Liz. She wants me to meet her after practice, then go out to dinner. I'm not too happy about showing my face at the court again, but I'm excited about the idea of chowing at China Moon.

Practice is still going on as I crutch half a block to the court. I consider waiting across the street for Liz, but I could really use a place to sit, and some water. It's hard to get a good grip on the crutches when your hands are all slimy and it's ninety degrees outside.

I try to slide onto the bench unnoticed; pretty impossible when you're sporting an aluminum pole under each arm. Maria's catching her breath on the side of the court. "Did you hear about Kate?" she says to me.

"No, what?" *She came here looking for me with a shotgun and her bully of a boyfriend?*

"She got sent home."

"Doesn't surprise me. I knew she'd snap sometime."

Maria laughs. "It wasn't her mind that snapped, it was her shoulder. The minute she got on the court, she was practically crying. Coach sent her home and told her to ice it. Can't come back without a doctor's note."

I wipe the sweat from my forehead. "How did she do it?" What I really want to ask is, was she hit by lightning? Is there a charred mark on her forehead? I'm feeling really guilty over this. Did I will death upon her? No, if I had special powers I would've offed her after our first encounter.

"She said she slipped on her brother's skateboard, but I have my doubts."

"You think she did it in on purpose?"

Coach blows her whistle and everyone scurries to pick up the balls.

"No, I think Bulldog roughed her up a bit," Maria says. "But you didn't hear it from me." She clams up.

"Wow, are you sure?"

"I'm no detective, but the evidence points that way." She quickly goes to help the rest of the team.

"Serves Thunder right," I mumble, but immediately take it back. She may be a total bitch, but her bulldog has the eyes of a serial killer.

purple forever

Liz doesn't look too good, and I'm not talking about the sweat dripping from her forehead or her frizzed-out hair. "Let's get out of here." She grabs my arm. I lose my footing and step down on my sore foot.

"Ouch, you're dealing with a cripple here!" I stop her with a crutch.

"Man, sorry, I forgot."

"What's wrong?" I ask.

She keeps on walking. "We'll talk at dinner."

"What's the buzz on Thunder, then? Do you really think her boyfriend did it?" I trail behind her.

"As far as I'm concerned, she deserves it." When Liz's mad, she'll snarl at an old lady crossing the street too slow.

"Yeah, but that guy gives me the creeps." I know we shouldn't judge people on how they look, but he would totally get the part of the asshole boyfriend in any made-for-TV movie.

"So, she gives me the creeps." Liz holds the door to China Moon open.

The restaurant is always busy; it doesn't matter that it's not even five yet. We get the last table in the back. The lights are dim and the azure walls are soothing.

I don't even look at the menu. "Do you want to do the usual?" I ask Liz. We always get an order of beef lo mein and egg rolls to share.

"Sure." She stares at her cell phone.

"So what's going on?" Her day couldn't possibly be worse than mine.

"I've left Harry two messages and he hasn't called me back yet."

"That's it?" This is *so* not like Liz. She must've fallen for him hard. "When did you last talk to him?"

"Last night. Right before dinner."

The waiter comes over and takes our order. He places a bowl of crispy noodles on the table, so I dig in. Liz doesn't budge.

"It hasn't even been twenty-four hours since you last spoke," I say. "Maybe he's busy."

"But he said he had the day off. Besides, he was supposed to call me back last night."

"Maybe he got busy later." I grab a handful of noodles. "I'm sure there's nothing to spaz about."

Liz pulls one noodle from the haystack and bites it

slowly. "Yeah, but he sounded weird when we spoke, like he wasn't busy but didn't want to talk to me either."

I reach over and shake her. "Liz, listen to yourself. You're not making any sense. Remember, you're the girl that doesn't take crap from anyone."

She laughs. "Yeah, you're right. I must sound pretty pathetic."

The waiter brings our waters and egg rolls. "Your food will be out in a few minutes. Anything else I can get you?"

"A new boyfriend," Liz says dryly.

The waiter opens his mouth but doesn't speak. I'm sure this is not the response he was expecting.

"Don't listen to her." I wave off her comment with my hand. He doesn't, and runs away.

"So now I'm crazy and a loser." Liz shakes her head.

"Oh no, you can't be worse off than me."

"Why? What happened?" Liz douses her egg roll with duck sauce.

"Ugh, I don't even know where to begin, but basically I was having a nice conversation with Graham at the gallery when my dad showed up late. I was pissed at him because he sold my favorite painting behind my back. I sort of blew up in front of Graham. I got so mad that I left the two of them there. Alone."

A little *ooo* escapes from Liz's mouth.

"I told you it was bad. He must think I'm a big fat baby."

The guy at the table next to us is feeding his girlfriend

soup. He even blows it cool before it reaches her lips. And he's cute, too. God, some people have all the luck.

"Did you say anything really obnoxious?" Liz asks.

"It's all one big blur, but Graham was right there when I came down on my dad. And I think he has a girlfriend and I made fun of her name."

Liz's eyes bug out. "Your dad has a girlfriend? Wow, that's great. I mean, for him." She takes a bite of her egg roll.

In the five years Liz and I have been friends, she's never seen my dad with a woman. Sure, he's gone on a few dates, but nothing worth mentioning. So I guess, technically, she's right—this is good news. For him.

"Yeah, I saw her one time at the gallery. Her name's Helga."

"What is she, a four-hundred-pound mud wrestler?" Liz laughs.

"Actually, I hate to admit it, but she's not bad looking. Petite with short blond hair. Pretty buff. About my dad's age."

"Really? Nice to meet you, I'm Helga," Liz says in a breathless voice.

"What a coincidence, because I'm Helga too." I hold out my hand and make kissy sounds.

Then we both crack up, big time. Tiny bits of egg roll fly out of Liz's mouth and I spray the table with crispy noodle residue.

I wipe my face with a napkin. "I bet Helga has better table manners than us."

Liz's cell vibrates on the table. "Maybe that's her calling right now." She looks at the phone and a big smile spreads across her face. "It's Harry," she whispers, like he can hear her.

"Well, answer it."

She pushes the phone aside. "No, he can wait. I'm busy."

The waiter slides the lo mein onto the table and gives us new plates.

"Are you sure you don't want to call him back? I don't mind." I spear the tower of lo mein with my chopsticks and manage to get some noodles onto my plate.

"No, I want to hear about Graham, how it was before your dad interrupted you guys."

"Oh my God." I put my chopsticks down. "It was magical. I felt totally relaxed with him, like I've known him all my life. We talked about deep stuff, my mom, his family, and he looked hot, even in purple."

"He wore purple?"

"Just his T-shirt, but on the purpleness scale, it was Barney purple."

"Barney?"

"You know, Barney. He's your friend, he comes from your imagination…"

Liz crosses her eyes. "You're weird."

"Me? Weird? Don't tell me you don't remember that show."

"There are some things I try to block out." Liz digs into her noodles. "So maybe purple is the new color for the season. I mean, a few years ago who would've thought guys would be wearing pink."

"Yeah, maybe. Purple is the color of royalty." I shrug. "So, do you think I should dye my hair maroon to get him to notice me?"

"No more hair dye, Princess Cassia." Liz shakes her hand. "Put some makeup on and you'll be all set."

"That's if he'll still talk to me."

"Call him tonight and ask him out to dinner tomorrow."

"I dunno. What if he says no?"

"Then I'll cast an evil spell on him and make his dick stay purple forever."

I nearly choke on my food. "Liz, you're so gross sometimes. But I love you anyway."

"Thanks, I try." Her phone goes off again and this time I make sure that she answers it.

meat pie ufo

It dawns on me, when I crutch into the condo at seven thirty after eating with Liz, that Dad said we'd have dinner together tonight. I never answered him, but still, you'd think he'd be here, slaving away in the kitchen. I'm stuffed, so it's a good thing he's not here. Plus, I'm pissed at him.

Only when I get out of the shower at eight thirty do I realize he is home. I put on a pair of crimson pajamas, actually the top from one set and the bottom from another, and plunk down in front of the TV.

"Ah, *ma jolie*." Dad's standing in front of me, holding a spatula and wearing the apron I bought him last Christmas. *Kiss the Cook*. Nice try.

I don't feel pretty, so I don't answer him. Instead, my eyes are locked in a dead heat with Will Jackson from the new show *Splitsville* until he turns to kiss his girlfriend.

Dad finally gets the picture and heads back to the kitchen. "Dinner will be ready in five, *ma cherie*."

I look at the clock on the DVD player: 8:50. Does he think I've waited this long to eat?

As the credits are rolling on *Splitsville*, Dad calls me to the kitchen. The table in there only has two seats, so I guess there's no chance someone else is going to save me.

Even though I'm still pretty full from China Moon, the food does smell good, so I shuffle over to the kitchen without my crutches.

I pick at my ravioli and watch Dad slurp down his.

Finally he looks up from his plate. "Aren't you hungry?"

"It's a little late." I point to the microwave clock. "I ate with Liz at five."

"Yeah, I tried to get out of the gallery early today, but it got very busy."

"Sure." I make an impression in the ravioli's skin with the tines of my fork.

Dad gets up to refill his plate. "So, did you see all the construction going on at the new high-rise? Those apartments are going to be svelte."

"Svelte?" He's definitely trying too hard to make everything seem normal when really we're less than two weeks away from Mom's fortieth birthday. Which, I just realized, happens to be on the same day as our most important basketball game—the game that decides whether we make the finals or not.

"Yes, it means…"

I clank my fork down onto the plate. "I know what svelte means, but nobody uses that stupid word anymore. It's embarrassing."

"You can take a man out of France, but not France out of the man." Dad laughs so hard I think he's going to pop a vein in his neck.

I cover my face with my hands and shake my head. *Urggh.* What does Graham see in him?

Dad holds up a ravioli with his fork. "Ravioli is an amazing thing. If you let it boil a second too long, it will burst, and a second too short, it's not edible. And it's no good the second day."

I push my fork deeper into the ravioli's skin. I pierce through to the other side. "Your daughter's no good the second day either," I blurt out.

Dad's patting his chin with a cloth napkin, and then it just falls to the ground. "Listen, Cassia. Is this about the painting in the closet?"

"No, it's about the skeletons in the closet."

Dad's jaw drops. I can't believe I said that. I can hear Liz cheering me on in the background: *You go, girl!* But I can hear Lucien in the other corner: *Your dad loves you more than you'll ever know.* But I'm tired of this charade. It's bad enough growing up without a mom, but it's even worse with only a few memories to hold on to.

Dad struggles for words. "Ahh, Cassia, I…I…I…"

Then the doorbell buzzes. Whoever it is got past security downstairs.

Dad eyes the door, then me. "Just answer it," I say, and get up from the table. I pick up his ravioli-stained napkin on the way out and throw it in the trash. Who has time to bleach it clean, anyway?

———

I turn on my stereo to drown out our mystery guest. Even if it's the cable guy, I don't want to see him. I think of calling Graham, and every reason not to. He hates me. He's watching reruns of *Cops*. He's having quiet time with his mom after his little brother goes to bed. There's a purple sale at Macy's…I stop after that one and dial his number. At this point my day couldn't possibly suck any more than it already has.

"Psychic hotline," the person on the other end answers.

"Huh?" I plunk down at my desk. "Oh, sorry, wrong number."

I'm about to hang up but the voice stops me. "Cassia? It's me. Graham." He laughs. Guess I threw my sense of humor away with the cloth napkin.

"Oh, right," I say, flustered. "I wanted to apologize for today. Sorry I blew up at my dad in front of you."

"Don't worry, I have parents too." I hear a soft knocking on my bedroom door. What happened to the mystery guest? I pretend not to hear. Then Dad whispers, "It was just Mr. Alvarez from 1201."

Phew. Hell-ga doesn't have an in with the doorman.

"Right." I swallow hard. "*I* only have one parent."

"I didn't mean…"

"It's okay. I know you were just trying to make me feel better." I hear Dad clomping back down the hall.

"It was stupid of me to show you the painting in the closet."

I straighten out the collection of ceramic dogs on my bureau. I arrange them in order from smallest to biggest. "I'm glad you did. My dad and I have gotten by for so long mentioning my mom as little as possible. I'm sick of it. I want to know everything about her."

"Well, your dad seemed pretty shaken up. Don't be mad, but I told him you were upset about the unfinished painting in the closet. He kept on saying he thinks about finishing it all the time."

How can I be mad at Graham? He was only trying to help.

"I'm not mad." I pick up a pencil from my desk and start doodling hearts up and down the margins of my notebook.

He takes a deep breath. "Good, because I didn't know what else to say. Lucien came by after you left and they were talking about a time when all four of you went to the beach. Your dad took a whole roll of film of you and your mom. Your mom got so annoyed with the camera that you guys threw wet sand at him and chased him all over the beach."

I laugh. "We packed the wet balls of sand tight and

called them meat pies." I scribble a meat pie on the page and a smaller one next to it. They look more like UFOs.

"You're making me hungry," Graham says.

"I can do that to people," I laugh.

"I knew there was something different about you."

"For real?"

"Yeah, sure. So many girls I've known turn out to be superficial. All they care about is looks. You're much deeper than that. Nice."

I'll ignore the "so many girls" part and focus on me. He said I'm deep and nice. "Thanks, I think."

"Trust me, it's a compliment."

My heart beats fast. It's now or never. "Hey, do you want to grab a bite to eat tomorrow?"

"Where?" he asks.

"Well, I haven't thought about it, but…" *China Moon, third table from the back where the light is dim, but we can still stare into each other's eyes. The perfect table for a kiss, far enough away from the kitchen and right in front of the statue of a Chinese dragon. Somehow I think this may bring good fortune.* "Let's say China Moon, tomorrow at seven."

"Oh, man, I totally forgot, I can't go…"

But before he can finish, I cut him off. "Maybe another time." I kick the side of my desk. *Ouch, not a good idea when you're barefoot and your other foot is already damaged goods.* I should've listened to my inner voice. I'm not his type. I only met him because of my dad, so why would he be interested in me?

"How about Wednesday? Same time, same place?"

So maybe there is an inkling of hope for us, Cassia and Graham. Cinderella and Prince Charming. Romeo and Juliet. Vanilla and Chocolate.

"Great," I say quickly, before he takes it back.

I can't believe he said yes, just like that. I was really beginning to think it was all about my dad, that I should've started off the conversation by luring him with promises of a sneak peek of Dad's early sketches, his college transcripts, and his prize possession (an autographed Picasso lithograph).

I hang up the phone and stare down at the piece of paper. At the meat pie UFOs. My smile seems to stretch for miles. "Mom, you'd really like Graham," I say aloud, just in case one of those flying saucers can transport the message to her.

mud stains

The best thing about today so far is that at my checkup,
the doctor told me I can ditch the crutches. I don't have
the green light to play ball yet, but he thinks in another few
days, I'll be back on the court. That means when I meet
Graham tomorrow for dinner, I don't have to look like the
Hunchback of Notre Dame hanging over a set of poles.

I can't believe we're really going on a date. Liz said it's
definitely a date, even if I asked him. She said the definition of a date is a girl and guy, who like each other,
going out alone. But I said, how do I know the feelings are
mutual, and she said he wouldn't have said yes if he didn't
like me. But I'm not too sure. We're talking about the
same guy who would kill to share a burger with my dad.

This morning, I managed to tip-crutch out of the
condo and avoid Dad. I didn't feel like rehashing where we
left off at dinner last night or, even worse, at the gallery.

I get off the elevator and fumble for my keys when the condo door swings open. "Hey, Dad," I say before I can stop myself. It's one in the afternoon. I thought he'd be gone by now.

He looks up a second before slamming into me. "Oh, I didn't see you. You're off the crutches. That's great."

"Yup." I wiggle my leg. "Surprised you noticed."

"Wonderful." He gives me a peck on the cheek. "I'll catch up with you later, *ma cherie*. I'm running late for a lunch appointment." He holds the door open for me.

"With who?" I don't budge from the threshold of the door.

His cell starts playing the chicken dance and he quickly flips it open. Who set that ringtone for him?

I'm still standing in the doorway, waiting for an answer. He walks down the hallway and throws me a backwards wave. I don't even know why I asked. The answer is obvious.

———

I veg out on the couch until it's time to leave for ceramics. Since I'm trying to get my ankle to heal as fast as possible, I'm stuck taking the bus. I'm really looking forward to class today, "to get to know the wheel" as Mr. Parker would say.

With the bus schedule, you can either be early for things or late. I choose early. "Hey, Mr. P, I mean, Eli, mind if I get started on the wheel?" I say as soon as I enter the art room.

He looks up from his computer screen. "Ah, Cassia. Sure, be my guest."

I peek over his screen. "No Photoshop transformations today?"

He laughs. "Nope. I'm writing a recommendation for an old student of mine. He's applying for an artist's grant. Lyle's a talented guy. He's going to have a couple pieces on display at La Reverie Gallery next month." He starts walking with me toward the back. "Some great works on display there. Ever been?"

"Sounds familiar," I say. Only about half the works belong to my dad. I give him a long hard stare. Mr. Parker couldn't have bought *Lady in Red*, could he? I don't want to talk about my dad, not now especially.

"See, I'm off the crutches." I smile.

He looks me up and down. "Indeed you are. You'll be back in top form in no time. Maybe even ready to play some ball next week?"

So they talked? Well, duh. Coach Parker is his wife. "Yeah. I kind of miss being on the court. Coach is good, too."

"Isn't she." He laughs deep. "Ceramics and basketball have a lot in common."

"They do?" I grab an apron, then sit down at the wheel and stretch my leg out. The pain from walking on it has kicked in, but it's not nearly as bad as when I first hurt it.

"Sure. You need good control for both activities. Keep your eye on the ball. Keep your eye on the clay…"

"Stay centered," I add.

"Exactly." Mr. Parker hands me a ball of clay. "If you need any help, give me a holler. I'm finishing up the recommendation before the rest of the students get here."

I nod that I've got it all under control and sink my hands into the wet clay. It's slimy and soothing at the same time. The fact that you can mold it into almost anything is amazing. It's hard to believe that humans could quite possibly be formed from the Earth's clay. Did God just sit around one day and create Adam and Eve from the very substance I hold in my hand?

I start the wheel and carefully guide the clay to the center. The clay spins to the side and I have to ball it back up and start over again. The classical music that is playing in the background is my focus today. I'm not going to think about my dad or my mom. This afternoon is mine.

I slap the clay down on the wheel again and this time it centers. I'm in synch with Beethoven, creating my own symphony. The naked clay and I engage in a stare off. Terra-cotta. The color of history. Ancient artifacts, thousands of years old, just dug up, don't look much different than the bowl I'm making. This piece will outlast me for hundreds of years and never lose its beauty.

Looking at it now, I don't even know if I want to style it up with glaze. The natural beauty of the clay is amazing, like a beautiful girl without makeup. Like a cake straight out of the oven, all golden brown, right before you add the frosting.

I know if I try to make an opening again I could ruin everything. "Eli," I call in a panicked yelp. "I need help."

I don't want to move my hands in case the whole thing leaps off the wheel like a flying saucer. Mr. Parker rushes over to me.

By now I'm in full panic mode, and I don't want to move my hands even a centimeter or I'll ruin what I already have. "I'm trapped!"

"You're forgetting rule number one," Mr. Parker says sternly.

"But my hands are wet, I've got the wheel at the perfect speed, my centering is dead on, and…"

"You're not relaxed."

"Oh, that again." I let out a puff of air and slink my shoulders.

"I'm waiting." Mr. Parker taps his fingers on the table.

I think about how this bowl is mine. I exhale once more, then ask Mr. Parker to show me how to make an opening in the clay again. It's overwhelming and I really want to make sure I don't miss a step. I try to appear as calm as possible, so that he believes me.

He tells me to use both hands. One hand must steady the other. I press my thumb into the middle of the mound. It starts off as a small hole, but quickly deepens as I press harder. Much better than my other attempts.

I'm using both hands to widen the center when a

vibration goes off in my pocket. It makes me jump and my right thumb slips. It takes a second to register that it's my cell going off. I quickly smooth out the ripple in the clay. Whoever it is can wait, unless it's Graham. He better not be calling to cancel our dinner tomorrow night.

Nia sits down and takes the wheel next to me. "Wow, you're really getting the hang of it. Don't tell him I told you, but it took Scott like ten tries to center."

"Really? Thanks." I look toward the front of the room and see Scott leaning over Mr. Parker's desk. "It's pretty intimidating, but I like it," I say.

"As soon as you get the opening you want, slow your speed." Nia dips her hands into the bowl of water. "Then it'll be much easier to pull up the walls."

My cell vibrates again, but I can't stop now. I'll lose my momentum. My thumb is stuck in the middle of the clay like that nursery rhyme where the boy sticks his thumb in the Christmas pie.

Nia and I sit side by side the whole class. She reaches over whenever I need a little guidance. I don't have to call Mr. Parker even once.

I'm one with the clay. We have a rhythm going like two singers in perfect harmony. Around and around it dances, securely on the wheel with my foot manning the pedal.

I'm ready to move to the next step—the walls—when the classroom door busts open. It's the burgundy lady, only now she's wearing sea foam. "Do you see her, Mr. Bernard?" she says, trying to catch her breath.

Mr. Bernard? Holy crap! It's my dad and he looks like he just swallowed a venomous spider. I let go of the pedal momentarily and the wheel skips a beat. My soon-to-be bowl goes flying and lands on the ground with a loud plop. My symphony ends on a deafening note. *Squashed Beauty.*

Dad stands in the center of the class, scanning the faces like a vulture scans the landscape for prey. His eyes stop on me and zoom in like a wide-angle lens. He lets outs a huge sigh of relief that I can hear all the way in the back. "Yes, that's her," he says, pointing to me.

All heads turn. Suddenly, ten pairs of eyes shoot me sympathy missiles. Dad thanks the burgundy lady and walks toward me, pounding the linoleum with each step. I can't move. Not even to pick up my mush of clay. What's he doing here? And why is he so pissed off all of a sudden? Mr. Parker is a few steps behind him. What does he think? Dad's some kind of deranged psycho who might go postal any minute?

Mr. Parker and Dad speak in a whisper. I can't make out what they're saying, but I can tell Dad's apologizing for barging into the class. He's wearing his cheddar-yellow T-shirt that says *Got Cheese?* and has sweat stains under the armpits. How embarrassing. No matter how much Shout I put on his shirts, I can never get the pit stains out.

Dad's standing in front of me now. "Cassia, I was looking all over for you." His face is red. I don't know if it's from the heat or anger or a combination of both, but I'm not sure if I want to know the answer.

"Why? What happened?" I gasp.

Dad tucks his head into his chin. "I thought I'd surprise you and go to your basketball game today. When I didn't see you there, I got worried."

Worried? Most of the time he has no idea where I am and now, when he actually looks for me, he's worried? Puhleese!

"But Dad, I just got off my crutches today. I can't play yet."

I notice Nia has left her wheel and is cleaning up my mess on the floor. I mouth, "Thank you." She gives me a quick smile and transports my now-defunct bowl to the bin of recycled clay. Hopefully it'll get better treatment from another potter.

"Didn't think about that." Dad shakes his head. "I asked a few people watching the game and they had no idea where you were."

"Liz's mom knew I was here," I say to the wheel.

"She eventually saw me and told me where to find you."

I stare down at my hands. They're stained with dried, cracked mud. Worse than any of the clothes Dad's ever left in the dirty-clothes hamper. "Oh. That's good."

"You still should've told me that you were here." Dad sighs.

I throw my hands up. "Why?" My words hang in the air.

I quickly realize that Dad and I are the only ones talking, and that everyone in the room can hear us.

"Let's get out of here," I say.

Dad thanks Mr. Parker for his hospitality and I follow him out.

"Call me Eli. I'm a big fan of your work," Mr. Parker replies.

Dad pats him on the shoulder. "Stop by La Reverie any time, Eli."

"I should've put the two names together," Mr. Parker says to himself as we make our way out.

After he shuts the door, Dad pulls me by the arm and says we'll take a taxi and talk at home. But we don't even make it to the corner where the taxis usually line up.

"You're limping," Dad says. "Let's stop here."

We plop down on the first bench in the Spirited Gardens, a block from the Y. It's a little garden that a widower set up after his wife died back in the 80s. The place is small but beautiful, and for the most part goes unnoticed. I've never seen more than one or two couples here. Today, there's nobody.

Dad opens his mouth to speak first. I know he's composing his words. He can paint anything, but when you ask him to talk, he's tongue-tied.

I'm not at a loss for words. I know what I want to say. Have wanted to say. I'm tired of pretending everything is fine. "Why don't we ever talk about her?" I blurt out.

"That's what this is all about?" He crosses his legs.

"Yes," I yell, but then am not quite sure. "And no. I mean, we tiptoe around our feelings. But I didn't tell you where I was because you never asked. Where did you think I was when I couldn't play ball all these days?"

Dad fumbles with his cigarettes. I shake my head and point to the hand-painted *no smoking* sign behind him. Tiny daisies surround the letters. The daintiness of the flowers and harshness of cigarettes make such a weird combo.

Dad shoves the pack back into his pocket without turning around. "I thought you were taking it easy at home or going out with your friends."

"That's your problem. You always assume things instead of asking."

He presses his fingers against his temple. "Time always seems to escape me. There are not enough hours in the day."

"That's your excuse for never coming to any of my games before?" I lean forward and rest my elbows against my thighs.

"I had every intention to, but things got in my way. I know that's no excuse—that's why I showed up today."

"A bit late," I scoff.

"I realize that, Cassia. Will you just give me a chance?"

"But you're always absorbed in your work. I feel like you never have enough time for me."

"No, no." He shakes his head. "You come before my art. Always."

"But even when you're here, I feel like you're somewhere else."

"I'm working on being a better listener. You have my

full attention now." He looks me straight in the eye. His eyes are like soft-serve ice cream. Mine are as hard as ice.

"I'm not even sure if you know anything that's going on in my life."

"I want to know everything that's going on with you. You're the most important thing to me. From the moment you were born, I fell in love with you. Your mother used to say that if I stared at you any longer, there would be nothing left to paint." He cups his hands and looks me in the eyes. "Sorry I've been distracted."

"It's her, Helga, isn't it?" I grit my teeth as I say her name.

"Her what?"

"Has she been what's distracting you?" I don't look at his face. I just can't. Instead, I turn to the bush next to me and pick at the purple flowers.

"Listen, Cassia, she's important to me, but not in the same way *you* are. My love for you goes deeper than anything I've ever known." His eyes are melting. "But I like Helga. Is this about me dating?"

"Part of it." My head's pounding. "There's so much that's been building up. Unresolved stuff."

"Start from the beginning," he says gently.

"Why don't we talk about Mom?"

Dad's eyes follow a fluffy black cat that scurries through the garden. It's feet pitter-patter along the paved area. Dad is still.

"Well, in the beginning, it hurt too much. Everything reminded me of her. How much I missed her. I was scared…it seemed easier to keep it inside. I thought you were young enough when she died that it didn't affect you."

I stand up. "But it did, Dad. Maybe not in the same way as you because I didn't know what reminded me of her. I wasn't sure if she hated lemons or loved them. If she took two spoonfuls of sugar in her tea or one. But even though Mom was gone, I wanted to be reminded of her. Desperately. For six months I sprayed my feet every morning with *Lilies of the Nile*, her perfume. I sprayed my feet so I could keep the smell just for me. I didn't want to share my memories of her with anyone, so mostly I kept quiet, too."

Dad's eyes are wet. His lashes are sticking together. "I'm so sorry, *ma cherie*. I didn't realize that my sadness and guilt were taking such a toll on you."

Now I'm in tears, too. It takes only seconds for my tears to become full-blown blubbering. I can't stand to see my dad cry. For a long time I thought his stoic attitude mirrored the way he felt inside, but now I know that's far from the truth. He missed her so much that he wanted to protect me from the hurt he lugged around with him every day.

I lean over and hug him. My dad. The man that loved my mother with all his heart. My tears leave a wet spot on the shoulder of his yellow cheese shirt.

"I'll finish the painting of you and your mother. I promise," Dad whispers into my ear.

His words leave a smile on my face.

ketchup sundae

You know you're pathetic when...you take over three hours to prep for a date that's not really a date, even if your best friend thinks so. Liz was really sweet and came over to help me get ready for my big dinner with Graham.

So here I am, standing in front of China Moon in complete date gear—full mask of makeup, black mini, and a lilac tank top. Purple is usually not my color of choice; I had to grab this one off the sale rack at the GAP, but if Graham likes purple, Graham gets purple. Now, if his favorite color was puke green, we'd have to talk.

Again, Liz means well but always goes a little overboard with her enthusiasm. So that's why I'm wearing mulberry glitter nail polish and eye shadow. I had to put my foot down when she wanted me to use a tube of Purple Pizzazz to fill in my lips. We compromised with Pink Vixen.

I check my cell clock—7:04—and poke my head

around the corner. No sign of Graham yet. Another five minutes and I'm gone.

Okay, now it's 7:07 and my makeup is starting to melt. I should've known he'd stand me up. He's probably too busy painting a self-portrait. He's so going to pay for this. I stare at my cell clock again as it changes from 7:08 to 7:09. *This sucks royally. I'm so out of here.* I'm walking past the door to the restaurant when it swings open.

"Oh, there you are. I was waiting inside," Graham says. He ushers me in.

"Oh, sure, right," I mumble. Only a real doofus, me, would wait outside when it's August in Miami.

Graham asks for a table and the hostess leads us to the back. Not to the romantic table by the Chinese dragon that I'd fantasized about (two burly guys in muscle shirts are at that one), but near the huge bamboo plant is good, too.

Graham looks down at my leg as we walk to the table. "No more crutches."

"Thank God."

"I guess you're ready for your first surfing lesson, then."

"I'd like that." I stretch my foot, trying to ignore the pain. Maybe I wasn't ready for heels just yet. "It's supposed to feel close to normal in a few days."

Graham pulls out my chair and waits for me to scoot in before sitting. Double points for being such a gentleman, especially on a non-date.

I'm surprised that he's wearing a crimson Polo shirt. Did he wear red because he knows it's *my* favorite? Or were all his purple clothes dirty?

Damn, he looks fine, like royalty. I heard that in China, the bride wears red instead of the traditional white. I wonder if the groom still wears black. Red symbolizes passion and lust and I'm *all* about that tonight. Graham is so hot, I can hardly speak.

"You hungry?" I manage to squeeze the words through the paste of Pink Vixen on my lips.

"Yeah, I am." Graham peeks over the menu.

"I mean, if you are, they have big portions here," I say, trying to sound like less of a Neanderthal.

I decide on chicken with cashews. Lo mein is a definite no for a first non-date. Graham orders Volcano chicken. Does that rule out a kiss at the end of dinner? I have no problems kissing a fire-breathing dragon.

Graham unfolds his napkin and places it on his lap. "You look really nice tonight."

"Thanks." I blush and instinctively tug the bottom of my shirt. "This is a new color for me."

Graham leans forward. "Good pick."

"Your favorite?" Could I be any more desperate?

He shrugs. "Yeah, you could say that. I like a lot of colors."

"Me too." I unfold my napkin. "I'm constantly analyzing everything by color. It's almost a sickness."

Graham leans forward. "Tell me more."

"See that guy over there in the pink shirt?" I gesture with a nod of my head.

Graham turns to his left. Then right. "Where?"

"One table over. Sitting with the blond lady. Can't

miss him." Not only is his shirt bright, but so is his skin. He's sporting a lobster sunburn.

"I see him now," Graham says. Maybe Graham could use a pair of glasses—he'd look cute.

"In his case, I think the pink is a sham. Pink usually means love and happiness. He's definitely a blue guy—cocky on the outside, insecure in the inside—but he chose this color because he thinks it will get him what he wants."

Graham looks perplexed. "What's that?"

"In her pants."

He bursts out laughing. "What does my shirt say about me?"

I twist the napkin on my lap. "It means you have confidence to go after your dreams."

Graham smiles big. Not a tooth out of line. "Huh. You could be right."

"Well, this is the first time I've actually seen you in red. You wear purple more."

"Right." His chin drops. "What's the scoop on purple?"

"Purple means imagination and balance. It's a favorite among artists. It can mean other stuff, too."

"Like what?"

"That you're trying to overcome obstacles in your life. But really, this isn't a science. I pick up a lot of info from books, the Net, my dad…" I'm blabbing on and on. I didn't even realize our food is sitting in front of us, untouched. "Should we eat?"

"Good idea." Graham unwraps his chopsticks, cautiously.

"Listen, I'm not trying to make assumptions about you because of what you wear." I pick up a cashew with my chopsticks. "I must sound like such an idiot."

"No, you're right." He hangs his head low.

Whoa. In an instant, all the red confidence has washed from his face. Maybe I've said too much. "Color doesn't define the person," I add quickly. "I'm sure there are many confident people who wear a lot of gray and many depressed people who wear bright red all the time."

"Yeah, but I do wear a lot of purple." His face sours. It's lost its usual glimmer. Maybe it's the lighting in here.

I splash some soy sauce on my plate. "So, it's cool."

"No, it's not."

Now I'm confused. "Why?"

"It's not cool if you *have* to wear it." He looks down at his food.

What, his mom works at the Purple factory? He belongs to a secret Barney cult run by crazed fans? "I don't understand."

"It's just that…" He takes a sip of his Coke. "No, it's nothing, really."

This time I reach across the table for his hand. "Graham, I told you about my mother, my father. Really, you can talk to me."

How did a conversation about purple get so deep? Did I miss something?

"I don't see the same way you do." He pushes the chicken around in his plate, then drops his chopsticks.

I so called it. "You wear glasses? I think guys in glasses are cool."

"I do wear contacts, but that's not it." He looks away from me, in the direction of the guy in the pink shirt.

He's fashion-challenged? Color dyslexic? The last thing I want to do is give the guy a complex. At the risk of sounding like an overzealous teacher, I say, "We all see things differently."

"No." Graham shakes his head.

"No?"

His green eyes are like stone walls. "I'm colorblind."

What? I'm stunned. Here I am, blabbing on about color like a know-it-all and he doesn't even know what I'm talking about.

"I'm so sorry." I put my hand over my mouth.

"Don't be. I do see color, just not the way you do. I see shades and hues. That's why I like bold, pure colors. Purple, even."

I lean forward and my hands graze his. "But that's what makes your artwork so unique. Your paintings say so much about life, and your use of texture is amazing."

"Thanks. I'm glad somebody thinks so."

"Whoever doesn't think you're an amazing artist is blind." Ah, way to stick my foot in my mouth. I slap my forehead. "Stupid thing to say."

"Relax." He reaches for my shoulder. "I know what you meant."

"How do you do it? I mean, without color?"

"I don't know any different. And I notice other things. Like, for example, ketchup and chocolate syrup look the same color to me, but they're clearly different consistencies. And for the record, I've never put chocolate syrup on my fries." He laughs.

I laugh too. "It sounds a lot tastier than a ketchup sundae. Wanna taste my cold cashew chicken?" I slide the plate toward him. He scoops a little off my plate and I take a bite of his Volcano chicken. I need a refill of Coke after a few bites.

I fan my mouth. "So, when did you know you wanted to be an artist?"

"I don't know exactly when, but I started drawing way before I started doing much else. The hardest part was convincing my parents."

"Why? Your talent is obvious."

"My mom couldn't see why a colorblind person would want to put themselves in the position of working with color. She doesn't know that there's so much more to art than color."

"Really?" I bite the inside of my lip, because she's not the only one.

I look over at the Chinese dragon. It's covered with a multitude of colors—crimson, jade, gold, black—but really, they could be any colors. It's the intricacies of the design and carvings that make it amazing.

"At first my dad thought being colorblind was something I could turn on and off. See this?" Graham points to the scar on his arm. "I was helping him with some wiring at a job site when I was eleven and I mixed up the red and green wires and burned myself. Had to go to the hospital. It wasn't until then that he realized I wasn't going to get over being colorblind. Before that, he thought it was a disease I would grow out of."

"It's amazing how parents can make themselves believe whatever they want. Just like my dad thinking if we don't talk about my mom, we'll both heal." I slide an amethyst bracelet, which Liz insisted I borrow, up and down my arm.

"I know what you mean. That's why I didn't let my parents stop me."

Then why am I such a coward? I forgot to mention that red symbolizes courage. Maybe that's why Dad uses a lot of red in his paintings. Why I choose it, too. "My mom's birthday is in eight days," I announce, like we're guests on a new talk show called *Spill It All*.

"That's awesome." Graham smiles. "You should do something for her. In her honor."

I nod. "I don't know what yet, but I plan to. This is a big one for her. For us."

The waiter comes over to clear our plates. "Any dessert?"

I look at Graham. He turns to the waiter. "Sure. Do you have fried ice cream?"

The waiter clears our plates and promises that the ice cream will be right out. *I'm in no hurry.*

"So, tell me about your ceramics class," Graham says.

I jerk my head back. "Who told you I'm taking ceramics?"

"I have my sources." He laughs.

"What? Did Dad post a status update on Facebook?" I scan his eyes for an answer but come up with nothing. "It's great. I really get lost when I'm at the wheel. It's much more intense than I ever imagined pottery to be."

"Enthusiasm will do that to you."

"What do you mean?"

"You know what it feels like to really love something, have passion for it?" Graham's eyes sparkle wide.

I've only been searching forever for that feeling. I've only had Ms. Cable's ominous words in the back of my head for months.

I stare down at my lap. At my lilac tank top. Purple doesn't go well with the yellowish tone of my skin. "No, I don't, actually."

He takes a sugar packet in his hand and taps it against the table. "It's that feeling you got when you realized you liked ceramics. That's what carries you from one project to the next."

"What if you don't have a real passion?" I look down at my hands, at my painted fingernails. I tried three different polishes of Liz's before I settled on the mulberry. "I get this grim image of myself in twenty years. I'm working behind the grill at Paloma's Diner, passionless. Then, after work, I go home to my efficiency in a seedy neighborhood. I eat tuna straight out of the can and share it with my cat."

"Hey, you'll find yours. You have to trust yourself first, though." Graham taps my arm with the sugar packet. He makes it seem so simple. "Besides, I'm sure you'd at least put the tuna on a nice plate!" He laughs.

"You're such a punk!" I laugh back.

The fried ice cream arrives. I let my spoon sink in. Then I slowly bring the ice cream and melted chocolate to my lips. Now this, I have passion for. I look over at Graham's scrumptious lips. Ditto. "You've got a speck of chocolate there." I point to his mouth.

He dabs with his napkin. "All gone?"

I shake my head no.

A sly grin emerges on his face. "Then help a guy out, will you?"

I lean across the table with my napkin. His grin is now a smile. I reach for his face—my lips are inches from his. My heart is beating like crazy. I focus on the redness of his lips. The color of courage. I let the pure-white napkin fall from my hand. I press the tip of my tongue against the spot of chocolate syrup on his bottom lip. He grips my shoulders and kisses me. His kiss is sweeter than the ice cream. Sweeter than the hot fudge.

Oh my freakin' God, I just kissed Graham Hadley. I have been struck by lightning a thousand times over. When the trembling subsides, I ease back into my chair and realize the edge of my shirt is now covered in ice cream. I dab at it like crazy with my napkin and Coke.

Graham takes the bill from the waiter. "See, and I'm colorblind, so I wouldn't have noticed the stain on your shirt if you weren't scrubbing at it like a mad woman."

I know that's not true, but it still makes me feel better.

lime and burnt orange

It has been two days since I kissed Graham at our non-date at China Moon, but I can still taste the chocolate from his lips. I hope he can't taste the Pink Vixen lipstick that was on mine. He left town the morning after our date to spend a week with his grandparents in Boca. It's only an hour away, but it feels like he left for another country.

I went to the doctor again today and he cleared me for all physical activity, but he did say to take it easy. How you do that in basketball is beyond me. I'm looking forward to playing ball again, to being in the center of the action.

I start jogging when I round the corner to the court. If I show up as a ball of sweat, then it'll look like I never left. Dad wanted to come to practice, but I told him to wait until the big game on Thursday. I definitely won't be in top form today, but hopefully my body will remember what to do.

Well, the sweat thing works and I have to take a big

swig of water as soon as I reach the court. A few people are already stretching.

"Hey, you're back." Maria stops to give me a high-five.

"Yeah, all better," I say, and walk over to the water cooler where Coach Parker is standing. I duck my head. "Uh, Coach, can you use another player today?"

She looks up from her roster book. "Cassia, hi, of course. I'm glad you're back, and just in time too. We have to win next Thursday to be in the finals."

I grit my teeth. "I know."

"Do you have a note from your doctor?"

I hand her my clearance paper. "I'm also wearing a brace, just in case."

"That a girl! A forward thinker. I like that." Coach looks past my shoulder, then waves to someone. "Hi, Julia, looking good." She quickly turns back to me and pats my arm. "Excuse me a moment, Cassia."

"Sure." I nod and turn around. The lady making her way over here looks very familiar. I jog my memory: blond hair, long skinny legs, early forties…

"Hi Patricia, how's your summer going?"

"Great. Keeping busy!" Coach says with her usual pep.

The lady looks at me. Her eyebrows cling together like they're holding on for dear life and her Cindy Crawford mole winks at me. "Cassia?"

"Ms. Cable?" I can only imagine what my sweaty face looks like.

"How's your summer going?"

All I manage to get out is, "All right."

She's wearing biking shorts and a tank top. Her hair is up in a ponytail and despite the sweat, she looks pretty. I'm used to seeing her in khakis and assorted button-down shirts in primary colors.

"Did you think about some of my suggestions?" she asks.

Did I ever! I want to scream out that she gave me a major complex, that I can't get her words out of my head. But something stops me. Maybe it's the way she's smiling and has her head cocked patiently, waiting for me to answer.

"Well, I've been playing basketball, and I took a ceramics class too. Plus, I've been drawing again."

I look out of the corner of my eye to see if Coach is going to rescue me, but she has her back to us. She's talking to Maria's mom. I'm stuck.

"That's lovely," Ms. Cable says. "Can you share some of your work with me?"

"Yeah, I can."

"Great. I hope I wasn't too hard on you, but now is the time to shine. Your junior year of high school is the most important year for colleges."

"Tell me about it," I grumble.

"I never said it was easy. Why don't you set up an appointment with me as soon as school starts up again."

"Okay." I nod. I guess I can give her another chance.

"You're a talented young lady." She smiles.

Whaat? Did I hear her right? Perhaps she said *you're as talented as a baby* or *you're a tacky young lazy*. Maybe she thinks I'm someone else? Could there be another Cassia at Dolphin?

"Cassia, get moving." Coach blows her whistle at me and winks at Ms. Cable.

I look back over at Ms. Cable before I run over to the court. She tells me to enjoy the rest of the summer.

I'm in a total fog when I find myself inches from Thunder's backside. I guess her shoulder injury was short-lived. She's stretching, in the last row. Usually Thunder's a front-row girl. Not today. I look at her long torso. I know she knows I'm here, but doesn't say anything.

Liz works her way toward me while we're doing squats. She leans over. "It's good to have you back on the court."

"Thanks. Sorry to have left you hanging with the elements." I point to Thunder.

Liz laughs and gives Thunder's back the finger.

"So, did you see who I was talking to a few minutes ago?" I ask.

Liz whips her head around; her ponytail flies. "No, who? Where?"

"Chill," I whisper. "Ms. Cable."

"Your counselor came to check up on you?" Liz gasps.

We break into a jog around the court with the rest of the team. "No, it looked like she was exercising. Probably going to the gym inside."

"So what's her deal then?"

I struggle to keep pace with Liz. "She was actually nice.

Said I was talented and told me to check in with her once school starts."

"Really?"

I wonder how Ms. Cable keeps all her students straight. Does she have case files on us, like the FBI does for criminals? Maybe she has a task force of minions doing the investigative work.

Coach blows her whistle at us. "Girls, enough chatter. Break up the party."

Liz moves ahead of me and I find myself jogging next to Maria. One more lap and we all hit the water cooler.

We quickly move on to lay-ups. I look for Baldwin, but decide any of his brothers will do. I grab a ball from the middle of the rack and wait my turn to shoot. Liz is right behind me.

"I thought you had a favorite," she says.

"How did you know?"

"Please, I know you." She rolls her eyes and laughs.

"Okay, then watch this." I run up to the basket, shoot, and miss.

I hear her laughing, but it's all good.

In a way it feels like I haven't missed two and a half weeks of basketball. Getting back in the groove isn't as hard as I thought. I'm not going to make any official announcements now, but maybe I'll try out for the school team this year. *Did you hear that, Ms. Cable?*

Thunder sneers at me when I fumble for the ball in our practice game. Otherwise, she's pretty much a mute, only whispering to Zoey now and then. The fear factor has dissipated after the rumor about Bulldog roughing her up. I mostly pity her now.

Coach blows her whistle and summons us to where she's standing, next to the water cooler. We all sit down, some on the bench, others on the grass.

"I'm really proud of you guys this season. Several of you I've known for a few years and others are new this year, but you've all played well as a team."

Ha, I want to say. *Have you forgotten about Thunder?*

Maria lets out a "wahoo" and soon everyone joins in. Coach waits until the noise dies down. "Let's kick some butt on Thursday so we can make it to the finals!"

Everyone cheers again and gets up to leave. Coach points to Thunder, then me. "I need to see the two of you."

So she did notice Thunder threatening me after all. *Hallelujah!* I know I said I didn't care, but after all, justice should be served. *Bon Voyage, Thunder girl. Apology not accepted and no end-of-the-year trophy for you, sucker!*

Coach gathers her belongings. "I wanted to have a little talk. If you're both free, we could grab a cold drink at Paloma's Diner."

I'm half expecting Ms. Cable to jump out from behind the tree with a grill scraper and announce that she's joining us for our first training at the diner. But she disappeared before practice even started, so maybe she had a change of heart. It's weird to agree to a little "talk" with your coach, but it's a hundred times better than if it was a school counselor.

"Sure." I shrug and so does Thunder. We follow Coach across the street. She buys us each a Coke and we sit down at a table. At least we're out of the heat.

We all pop open our drinks. Thunder abandons her straw and takes a huge swig; fizz rises out of her can. She wipes her chin with the back of her hand. "No offense, but why are we here, Coach?"

"I think you two have a lot in common, but this rivalry has to end." Coach scoots her chair closer to the table.

Something in common? That's like saying lime and burnt orange would be the perfect color combination for a prom dress. I nearly choke on my straw and soda escapes from my nose. Ouch, that hurt.

"Exactly." Thunder scoffs.

Coach doesn't seem fazed. "Sometimes we need to look beyond the superficial. You're both strong women, but each of you needs to trust yourself more."

What is it with this whole trust thing? First Graham, and now Coach? "What do you mean?" I ask.

"Well…" Coach points to me. "You're very talented, but you don't allow yourself to reap the benefits of those talents." I look over at Thunder. Her nose is all scrunched up and her freckles look like they're going to pop off any minute.

"In basketball?" I ask.

"Sure." Coach gives me a peppy smile. "But also in other things."

"Well, I really like ceramics." I swat at a fly hovering above our table.

"Then you should think about pursuing it," Coach says.

"But you can't have two passions." I shake my head. I've never seen Dad stray away from his art to "pursue" something else. Who ever thought of Monet taking up ballroom dancing or Picasso playing water polo?

A little boy at the table next to us squeals with delight. His older brother has a spoon hanging from the tip of his nose.

"Whatever gave you that idea? Look at me." Coach tugs at the whistle around her neck. "I'm a drama teacher during the school year and I coach intramural basketball in the summer."

Thunder and I both nearly jump out of our seats. "You are?" I say.

Coach raises her eyebrows.

My mouth forms the perfect O. "And Mr. Parker coaches football during the year?"

Coach lets out a guffaw. "Please, his idea of exercise is walking a block to Ben & Jerry's."

Thunder and I both laugh. I try to stifle my laughter by covering my mouth with the crook of my elbow, but Thunder lets it all out.

Coach smiles.

Thunder's face goes back to being lackluster. "This is B.S. I'm not creative like you guys. I can't even draw a stick figure."

Coach gives her the eyeball.

"Sorry," Thunder mumbles.

"Creativity comes in all forms," Coach says. "If you want to be a good ball player, you have to be creative."

"Let's face it. I'm not going to play professional ball when I get out of school." Thunder leans back and crosses her arms.

"And you don't have to." Coach reaches out to her. "You just have to allow yourself to try different avenues, to explore."

Thunder rubs her shoulder but doesn't make eye contact with either of us. She immediately resumes the crossed-arm position.

I feel compelled to rescue her. "Yeah, if I didn't get a total scare from Ms. Cable that I'd be working at a diner like this for the rest of my life, I'd probably be at home watching TV all day. Then I wouldn't have found out that I liked basketball, or ceramics either."

Coach claps her hands. "Exactly."

"Please, you've played before." Thunder looks at me like I'm Pinocchio reincarnated.

"No, really, it's the truth. This is the first time I've been on a real basketball team."

Thunder twists the tab of her Coke can round and round. "But you're a good player."

"Me?" I point to myself. This is the first time anyone's ever said that about me. Strangely, it feels good. *Watch out, there's a new Killer Cassia in town!* A chill goes up my spine. "But nothing like you. I thought *you* were intimidating, with all the baskets you make every game."

"You're both great players. And you should find your self-esteem on the court and in other endeavors," Coach chimes in.

"What are you saying?" Thunder rolls her eyes.

"That confidence does not come from relationships, but from within."

"This is corny," Thunder says.

I knew her little nice-girl act wouldn't last.

My eyes immediately dart over to Coach's face. *Go ahead, blast Thunder for being so rude.* But Coach doesn't bat an eye. "What makes you think that, Kate?"

"I dunno." Thunder shrugs. "I feel like people just give you that bull, I mean, speech, but they don't really give a crap about you. Like one of those feel-good therapists on TV. *Tell me how you really feel…*"

"Well, you make it hard for people to like you," I say. Wow, I can't believe I had the balls to say that. Two points for me! I just stood up to the Big Thunder. I look at her, but she doesn't respond. For once Thunder is speechless.

I turn to Coach, but she's twisting her wristband. This is the first time I've seen her hesitant. I hope she doesn't think I'm acting like a wench. Maybe she'd like to call Ms. Cable for intervention backup. She looks straight at Thunder. "Kate, nobody likes to be treated badly, and I'm sure Cassia agrees."

Thunder rolls her eyes again. "What are you talking about?"

Coach leans over and rubs Thunder's shoulder.

Thunder winces. "It was an accident."

I've got to say something. Even if Thunder is a bitch, she still shouldn't let Bulldog beat her up like that. I don't want to be interviewed after her death and say I knew something was going on, but I was too chicken to speak up.

"Why do you let him treat you like that?" I slide my chair back in case she feels like pouncing on me.

"Leave Ryan out of this," Thunder snaps.

"I'm here to listen," Coach says, then adds, "or we could talk afterwards."

Thunder slams her fist on the table but quickly jerks her arm back. "I said, leave him out of this. Ryan's a great guy. Best thing that's ever happened to me."

Talk about someone in denial. This is sad.

"Then why did he do that to you?" I point to her shoulder.

Thunder takes a deep breath. I watch her chest rise up and down. "He didn't do this. Or anything."

"Really," I say. Even I've seen all those episodes of *Law and Order* where the victim sides with her abuser, trying to protect him.

"I don't care if you guys don't believe me. It's the truth!" Thunder shouts.

Coach reaches out and places her hands on top of Thunder's. "It's only because we care about you."

"Yeah, well, you shouldn't." Thunder lowers her head.

I thought I had low self-esteem, but damn, hers is rock bottom.

"You're not *that* bad," I mumble.

Thunder looks up. Her eyes are cloudy. "I did it, okay."

Coach and I both look at her but don't say anything. What is she talking about? She beat herself up?

Thunder rubs her nose. "It was me. I punched Ryan and my shoulder snapped. It was such a stupid fight. But sometimes I can't help myself. I get so angry."

Thunder punched the half-ton bulldog? That doesn't make sense. What about his evil eyes? He had his arm around her so tight, that day I saw them walking to the court.

"But he looks so scary," I say.

"Ryan's a teddy bear. He cries at chick flicks." Thunder's face is red and splotchy.

I can't believe I felt sorry for this girl.

"But everyone on the team thinks…"

"I don't care what they think," she cuts me off.

"It's okay, Kate," Coach says.

"I'm a fucking bitch." Thunder shakes her head. "I screwed up. It's like something takes over and I can't stop myself. Sometimes I get so mad, I feel like my head is going to pop off." She digs her nails into the side of her arm.

Wow, this is totally messed up.

"It's great that you're finally opening up," Coach says. She sounds like such a natural. How does she know what to say to Thunder? I'm still in shock that she beat up on such a huge guy, even if she is 6'1".

"That's about the only thing. I've got all the charm of my old man. At least that's what my mom says." Thunder laughs. It's a deep laugh, not the kind reserved for jokes.

"Did he hurt you?" Coach asks.

"Yeah, but he's history. Ran out on us five years ago. Never seen him since. Wished him dead plenty of times."

Thunder releases her fingernail grip. The color slowly returns to her arm.

"I'm so sorry," I whisper. My dad's never even laid a hand on me. Not even when I've acted like a total brat.

"The worst thing is…" Thunder wipes the tears from her cheek with her palm. "I've done this before, taken my anger out on other people, on Ryan."

"I'm happy to get you help," Coach says.

"All right," Thunder complies. She didn't put up a fight. Maybe there is hope.

"Anything you want to say to each other?" Coach looks at me, then Thunder.

"You're an okay player, Cashew," Thunder blurts out.

I look at her. At her hollow brown eyes set a little too far back into her head. I guess this is her way of apologizing. Even if she is the bully, my sympathy for her doesn't change. She seems so lonely. She's still a victim. "Thanks. You too, Thunder."

"Thunder?" She looks confused.

Coach slams her hand on the table. "I'm counting on both of you for Thursday's game."

"You still want me?" Thunder asks.

"Absolutely." Coach nods. "We have some more talking to do, though."

I drain the last of my soda from the can and stand up. "What about ceramics?"

"Game doesn't start until five, after ceramics ends. Don't let that wheel wear you out, because you're both starters."

Kate and I look at each other and nod.

battle of orange and red

In a moment of weakness, I agreed to join Dad and Helga for dinner. Actually, Dad asked me four days ago, but now, ninety minutes before we're supposed to meet Helga at the restaurant, is when I start to panic. The plan is for me to meet Dad at La Reverie before we catch a cab to Athena's, a Greek restaurant about a mile from the gallery.

First off, I have no idea what to wear. I don't want Helga to think I'm just some dumb kid. I mean, if there is any remote possibility that she wants to continue to date my dad, she has to know he's *my* dad. I don't want some bossy control-freak woman barging into our lives thinking she can take over. That being said, I need to wear something that means business.

I'm leaning toward black pants and a solid shirt, like blue or green. I take out the silk aqua blouse that I save for Dad's art shows. Aqua usually means you have high ideals. Or I could wear the button-down baby-blue shirt that would be sure to lull Helga to sleep. Maybe then she'd keep her paws off my dad. Even though I feel glam in either of these outfits, I want to wear something that makes an impact. I need to show that I'm in charge. Red is the way to go.

I pull out a wine-colored tank top from my drawer, but it's ribbed and way too casual. I step into my closet and wade through a couple potential reds. Then I see it, at the very back—my little red dress from the painting.

It's simple, with a small ruffle lining the bottom. I haven't looked at it in a long time. Mom sewed it herself, on the same sewing machine that her mom had sewed her clothes on. She wanted us to match for the portrait. We had to stand completely still as Dad worked his magic. The wind on the balcony blew the backs of our dresses slightly, making the warm air bearable. Mom held my hand tight for what seemed like an eternity. Finally Dad said we could call it a day, that he would need us again when he got to the finer details. That day never came, because Mom died five days later. Not even all our love could plug up the pinpoint-sized hole in her heart.

I take the red dress from the hanger and run to Dad's bedroom closet, where he keeps an oversized box of Mom's personal things. In all the years since her death, I've never seen him take it out. However, I've sifted through it on especially lonely days, on days that I long for her companionship. I've never gotten to the bottom of the box. I didn't want the memories of her to come to an end.

The box is pretty heavy but I manage to pull it out and slide it across the carpet. I sit up against Dad's sturdy iron bed and inch it closer to me. I lift up the flaps and stare inside: jewelry, photos, journals, all things I'm dying to get my hands on. These are my mom's treasures—my treasures now.

My body is trembling—there's so much of *her* in this box. I know it sounds stupid, but I can feel her presence, even smell the scent of lilies she left behind. I stick my head in and inhale. Among the musty smell, there's still that flowery sweetness. I dig down deep until I feel something soft. I slowly pull it out. It's not the dress, but a red piece of cloth. I haven't seen this before, or if I have, I've ignored it. Is this the material Mom used to sew the dress? I slowly unfold it in front of me; it's the size of a bathroom towel. I hold it up to my little red dress. The fabric is the same. It's what an artist would call "pure red." It's what I imagine a designer would search for to make the wedding dress for the princess of China. I run the smooth fabric across my face and breathe deep. I remember this is what it felt like to be close to her, to feel her touch, her face as smooth as silk.

I get to the bottom of the box, but no dress. Where else could it be? I quickly glance at Dad's clock radio. Crap, I need to be at the gallery in less than thirty minutes and I still need to find something to wear. I take the fabric, an envelope of photos, and one of Mom's journals back to my room with me. The photos and journal will be safe under my pillow until I get home, even though I would rather stay here and devour them now.

I go with black pants and a black tank, then throw the red cloth over my shoulders. Still, my outfit is incomplete. Rummaging through my drawers, I come up with a tube of scarlet lipstick. I paint my lips and blot with a tissue. Maybe I should've worn this color to my dinner with Graham. Not that he would've noticed the difference from Pink Vixen, but I do.

I stare into the mirror. With the black hair and scarlet lipstick, Vampire Chick comes to mind, but I also feel like an adult. Scary. My cell is ringing. It's Dad. Figures he actually remembers we have to be somewhere when it comes to a date.

"*Ma cherie*, are you on your way?" he asks.

"I'm leaving in a sec." I peel myself away from the mirror and slip on a pair of strappy sandals with a small heel.

I'm at the gallery in less than fifteen minutes. Not bad for a girl recently off crutches.

"How's it going, kiddo? Don't you look gorgeous! Your dad will be out in a minute." Lucien pulls up a chair for me and we both sit down at his desk. He opens the drawer and offers me some Saltines. He knows me too well. Maybe they'll help calm my Helga jitters.

I pull a couple loose from the packet. "Thanks."

"I'm coming to your game on Thursday. Looking forward to seeing you back on the court." Lucien crumbles up a piece of paper and tosses it into the trash can.

"Lucky shot." I fiddle with the top desk drawer, sliding it open and closed. "I'm glad you're coming. In case Dad forgets."

"No, your father will definitely be there. I showed him how to program his cell to go off half an hour before he needs to be somewhere."

I lean back in my chair. "You did not!"

"It was either that or tie a string on his finger." Lucien laughs. "If it's any consolation, he was always a bit flighty…just a little more so after Bianca passed. She really kept him in order."

"I'm not marrying a guy without a personal secretary." I slam the drawer shut.

"That's going to be some event. Your wedding. But promise me you won't get married for at least another twenty years." Lucien pats me on the back.

I scrunch up my eyes and tilt my head.

"Okay, ten years."

"For now I'm focusing on non-date number two."

Lucien gives me a funny look. He's so easy to talk to, I forget he doesn't speak *Girl*. I hear the bathroom door swing open. "You're a good catch, kiddo," he says. "Your mother would be proud." There's nothing like having a pseudo uncle.

I get up from the desk and meet Dad halfway across

the gallery floor. His hair is fully gelled back and he's doused with cologne for the over-forty crowd.

"Cassia, you look so grown up." He smiles, then takes my hand and twirls me around. He sings the words softly, about the lady in red.

"You don't look too bad yourself." I smile back at him.

"For an old guy, right?" He puts his hand on his hip and gestures for me to link arms. "Shall we?"

———

We arrive at the restaurant before Helga, quite possibly a first for Dad. He talks to the host and picks his own table near the back. The tablecloths are white with cerulean embroidered flowers. Multiple chandeliers hang from the ceiling and the hardwood floor shines like the top of Mr. Clean's head.

Dad orders me a Coke, but I can't even take a sip. My stomach is queasy. Actually it's more a mixture of butterflies and swords. Butterflies for the jitters and swords to keep Helga away. Maybe I should tell Dad I'm not ready yet, that I need a little more time to let the idea of her sink in.

If there ever was a need for an escape door, this would be one of those times. A petite lady with a glowing tan and cropped platinum-blond hair walks toward us with a cell phone glued to her ear. She's wearing an orange linen dress with thin straps. She shoves her cell in her purse and waves in our direction. Even if I hadn't seen her before, I would know it was her. She has Helga written all over her face.

I think Dad senses my sudden urge to flee because he

rubs my back, then stands up to greet the lady in orange. I wonder what color she would appear to Graham. Poop brown, maybe? Perhaps he has the gift of seeing the truth.

Dad gives Helga a quick peck on the cheek and pulls a chair out for her. I don't move from my seat, frozen like a Popsicle.

Then she leans down and gives me a kiss on the cheek, too. "And you must be Cassia, even more lovely than your father described."

Hello? Didn't she see me at the gallery the night I saw her, or was she too busy groping my dad? Without defrosting, I manage to eek out, "Nice to meet you." I don't say "Helga" because the very mention of that name might send me into giggle spasms. I can't get the picture of Liz out of my mind breathlessly whispering "Hell-ga."

With her orange dress, Helga is supposed to bring the warmth of the sun to tame my ball of fire. She is supposed to be in control. Of course, maybe she's really a gray lady, dull to the core, but forced herself to put the dress on. Okay, a little dramatic, I know, but I've got my eye on this woman. One wrong move and she's out. I didn't spend a year in the fifth grade doing karate for nothing.

Let the battle of red and orange begin. May the best-dressed lady win.

lady in red

Helga and Dad share a bottle of red wine while I sip at my Coke.

"So, I hear you're quite the basketball player, Cassia." Helga dips a piece of focaccia bread into the bowl of oil in the center of the table.

"Kind of short-lived, since I sprained my ankle in the middle of the session." I tap the tip of my knife against the table, making a small indentation on the tablecloth.

"What about the game on Thursday?" Dad straightens out his collar.

"Yeah, but that's it, unless we make the finals. Then we could have three more games." Tap. Tap.

"I'd love to see you play. Mind if I tag along?" Helga's eyes twinkle. It doesn't take much to excite this lady. God, does she have to be such a poser? Who says I want her swooning over Dad while I'm trying to score some baskets? As if I need any more distractions during the game.

I tap my knife harder and faster against the table. I wonder if they can kick you out for annoying repetitive noises.

Dad clamps down on my wrist, abruptly ceasing my noisemaker. "Helga asked you a question, Cassia."

Man, I wouldn't have agreed to go out to dinner if I knew she was going to be all up in my business.

I wiggle free from Dad's hold, but I'm still gripping the knife. "It's really hot on the court, you'll sweat a lot." Probably melt like the Wicked Witch of the West.

"I played tennis for years. I'm used to sweat." Helga laughs.

Dad's leaning back in his chair, sipping his wine like he doesn't have a care in the world. How does he do that? Let everything go? I adjust my cover-up so it doesn't slide off my shoulders. This is the only piece of fabric that Mom saved. I can't afford to get it dirty. "Fine," I murmur. "But don't be late. Coach hates tardy people."

The waiter takes our orders. Dad picks lamb and Helga and I both ask for Greek salads. Surely, we can't have anything else in common besides our choice of dishes. I go to the bathroom twice before dinner arrives. Once because I really have to go and the second time to call Liz. I don't even wait for her to speak.

"Liz, she's so annoying. I'm not even going to say her name, but you know who I'm talking about."

"Your dad's girlfriend, I mean, friend…"

"Don't say that! She's the lady from Hell. All cheery and crap, wants to go to the game on Thursday."

"So what's the bad part?" Liz asks.

"Hello?" I want to smash the phone against the bathroom wall. Would do it, too, if I didn't remember that's how Liz broke hers. "It's totally fake. How could anyone be so happy about meeting some guy's daughter?"

Liz laughs. "If she gets too nice, then spill your drink on her or flick hot sauce in her eye."

I open the bathroom door and peek around the corner to make sure no one's listening. "I can't do that. You know how much it costs to dry-clean linen."

"Okay, then do the whole cold-shoulder thing. You're good at that."

"Thanks. I think." I look out at our table. The waiter is setting down plates of food. Dad waves at me. "Dinner's here. If you don't hear from me later, assume I'm dead."

"Don't forget, Graham's still alive," Liz says before I hang up.

Very alive. I wonder what he'd think of Helga. He'd probably like her. Think she was very interesting and friendly. Geez, nobody's on my side. I stomp back to the table. They're waiting for me, to eat.

"There you are." Dad seasons his dish with pepper. "Did you know Helga teaches an art history course at UM?"

"Yes. You already told me that." I stuff a wad of feta cheese into my mouth.

"I also co-own a framing business," Helga adds, like that'll pique my attention.

I let the cheese melt against my tongue before I answer. "Oh, that sounds fascinating."

Dad sets his glass down. "Actually, it is. Helga sells high-end, ornate frames. She contracts with museums and big corporations. Has met all sorts of neat people."

He's got me wrong if he thinks I'm going to jump on the I've-met-a-celebrity bandwagon. A celebrity to her is probably some old country singer with one foot in the grave or the prime minister of some never-heard-of-before country the size of a pea.

"My favorite Miami client is that actor from *Ocean's Eleven*, Matt Damon."

"He's all right for an old guy, Helga." There, I said her name. All in one syllable, though.

"Framer to the stars." Dad chuckles at his own joke.

Helga gently rubs Dad's shoulder. There she goes again with the touchy-feely crap. *Don't get too close, lady, or I might have to chuck a tomato at you.* "Jacques, you make me sound so important."

"Well, you are." He takes her hand and squeezes it.

I clear my throat really loud and slurp my Coke like I'm trying to sip up the entire ocean floor.

Dad and Helga both laugh. I don't find anything funny. My blood's overheating. The waiter comes over to check on us. Helga fake-smiles and tells him we're doing well. Well for a dead fish maybe, but not for me.

I keep my hands busy slicing through the mound of lettuce on my plate. I'm cutting it into tiny rabbit-sized bites like Mom used to do for me when I was small.

Dad nudges me with his elbow. "What?" I snap.

"Don't you want to ask Helga anything else about herself?" There is a drop of oil on his white shirt sleeve. I'm not going to tell him; he'll have to figure it out for himself.

I roll my eyes. "Dad, if you haven't noticed, I'm trying to eat."

"Cassia, what's gotten into you?" He tugs his left earlobe. Is he aware that he's sending out the Jacques Bernard SOS signal?

I slam my fork down with a clank. "Me? I'm not the one trying to be Mr. Perfect, kissing ass to impress some woman."

Dad's face drops. He sets his knife and fork down on his plate. "You're being very rude to our guest."

"Our guest?" I push my chair back from the table and fold my arms. "You mean, *your* guest."

The waiter clears our plates and leaves a few dessert menus on the table.

Silence.

More silence.

I don't know about them, but I'm enjoying the silence.

"Are we ready?" Dad finally speaks.

"Ready to get out of here." I grit my teeth.

Dad gives me the death stare. Helga smiles at him and says, "All teenagers would rather be anywhere but with their folks."

"Hurumph." I flip open my menu. "Yeah, I'll get something." Maybe some chocolate will ease the pain. I flag down the waiter and order a slice of SINsational chocolate cake.

"I've got a big surprise for you, Cassia," Dad says after the waiter finishes taking our dessert orders.

I pull the red fabric tight around my shoulders. I'm skeptical, very skeptical. "What?"

"Well, I should mention that Helga is part of it too," Dad adds.

She shakes her head no at him. Her orange glow ignites my fire until I feel like my face is a wild blaze burning out of control. The flames quickly spread until my whole body is burning up. Not even a fleet of fire trucks could save me now. "No way!" I yell. I mean, really yell. I get up from my chair so fast that it falls to the ground. It's so unfair—I just met the lady and now they're getting hitched! "It's too soon!" I run from the table, past all the other diners, out the front door.

Dad calls my name, but I can't stop. The smoke has filled my lungs. I can't breathe. I need fresh air.

My back is pressed against the stucco wall of the restaurant as I try to catch my breath. I can't believe them and their sick plan. What's next, they're catching a plane to Vegas so they can get married by Elvis in the Chapel of Love? Make me puke!

A fire truck races by. I wave my hands hysterically. "The fire's over here," I shout.

I see Dad storming toward me. His untucked shirt flaps as he runs.

"Cassia, what is it?" Dad pushes my hands down.

My eyes well up and tears flow freely like a broken hydrant. "How can you marry her?" I blubber.

"Relax, *ma cherie*." Dad is still holding me. "We're not getting married. Let's take things one step at a time."

I wipe my face with the cover-up before I realize what I'm doing. "Then what's the grand announcement for?"

"I have a gift for you." Dad removes a sticky strand of hair from my cheek.

I'm still trembling on the outside, but elated on the inside that they're not getting hitched. At least not for now.

An older couple walks by and whispers. They were sitting at the table next to us. I don't care if they're talking about me. They know nothing about my life.

Dad reaches into his pants pocket and pulls out a rubber eraser. He takes my hand and places it inside.

"This is my gift?"

Dad laughs. "No, something to tide you over. Now please come back inside."

I thumb the eraser, then look up at him. At the few small creases extending from each eye. To my mom he's probably forever young. I wonder if she knew how much he truly loved her. Does she know how much we both miss her, how we would do anything to feel her presence? I look up at the sky. The setting sun reveals the night's colors—crimson, orange, and mauve. I imagine Mom looking down at us. *I'm with Dad now,* I want to say. He grips my hand tight and I follow him inside.

Helga hasn't moved. She must be one nutty lady to stick around. Who wants to date a guy with a psycho daughter? She smiles big when we get back to the table.

"Sit down and I'll get it," Helga says. She walks to the other side of the restaurant.

"Does she have to be here?" I ask Dad.

He puts his hand on my shoulder. "Trust me, Cassia, she's a good woman."

"For you maybe." I roll my eyes.

He doesn't answer, but I can tell from the look in his eyes that he's done pleading with me.

Helga returns to the table with a large package wrapped in Bubble Wrap and brown paper. A painting, no doubt. Don't tell me she's a budding artist, too. And if it's a portrait of her and Dad, I'm going to punch a hole through the center.

Dad moves the condiment basket from in front of me and lays the painting down. Then kisses me on the cheek. "For you, *ma petite fleur.*"

He hasn't called me his little flower in a long time. Not since I used to climb into his bed when I couldn't sleep. He would tell me to close my eyes and he would sprinkle me with magic seeds. The seeds would help me grow, he said. No wonder I have such big feet!

I slowly unwrap the package. First I remove the masking tape, then the Bubble Wrap, and finally the brown paper. I take a deep breath to prepare myself for what might be inside.

My heart thumps.

No he didn't!

It's so beautiful, and the new frame is amazing, like spun gold.

"Wow," I say, and look up at Dad. He's all smiles.

A little girl with long strawberry-blond hair stops at our table to stare at the painting. I don't blame her. I give her a mini-wave, but her mom tells her to keep moving and pulls her toward the bathroom.

"*Lady in Red.* Dad, why couldn't you just tell me you were having her reframed?"

Helga and Dad both take their seats again. Dad reaches across to me. "There's more to this painting than you think. Look at the woman's face."

I pause and stare at it. "You want specifics? Okay, first off, she's beautiful. She's wearing sunglasses, has a long nose. I don't know."

Dad purses his lips. The words flow from his mouth in slow motion. "It's…your…mother."

I don't even try to hide my confusion. "Huh? That's impossible."

"When I first met Bianca, she'd dyed her dark hair

blond. This is your mother, and you look very much like her. That's why I wanted you to have it, because you're also my lady in red."

I run my finger down the slope of my nose. My long nose. I wish I too had a pair of sunglasses to hide behind, because my eyes are welling up again and I don't know how long I can keep the tears from spilling out.

"But why give it to me now?" I gulp back the tears.

"I was going to surprise you with it on Thursday. Her birthday. But I didn't think it could wait. And when I told Helga about it, she offered to have it reframed."

"It's so beautiful. Thanks so much, Dad." I get up and hug him. "And you too, Helga. I've always thought the frame kind of sucked."

She smiles, then says, "You truly are the lady in red. That wrap is amazing on you."

"My mother made us dresses out of it. This is the leftover cloth."

Suddenly Helga rises from her seat. "You know what, I really ought to run. So if you don't mind, I'm going to leave you two here." She takes some bills out of her wallet and tries to hand them to Dad, but he pushes them back at her.

Dad plants a kiss on her cheek and whispers, "Thanks." I watch as she walks away. The sun gets smaller and smaller, then disappears out the front door. But I can still feel her warmth, especially the glow she left on Dad's face.

I stare at the painting. At my mother. "Dad, I can't wait to bring her home."

His eyes are wet too, but his smile is what really powers his face. "She would be so proud if she could see you now. Cassia, you've grown into an amazing young woman. So smart. So talented."

"But not like you, Dad." I shake my head. "You've been painting since you were three. I only started ceramics this summer."

"It doesn't matter when you start something, or if you start it and hate it six months later. Passion comes from within." He points to his chest. "It just takes different forms. I only wish I was as gifted as you."

I screw up my face like a jigsaw puzzle. "Yeah, right."

"To be able to pick up a basketball, then work your hands at the wheel." He takes my hands in his. "Look at the power you hold."

"Yeah, I have large hands." Great for gripping the basketball, not so good for finding a pair of gloves that fit.

"Just like your mother." He smiles.

"She had big hands too?" I look down at the painting. Her hands are at her sides.

"Do you think she wanted me to paint her hands all stretched out?" Dad laughs.

I pull the cloth wrap tight around my shoulders again. I have to ask. "Dad, where is the dress?"

He sighs. "I know you want me to work on the balcony painting, and like I said, I will. Soon. I promise." His eyes are full again.

This time I reach out to him. "Dad, I know you will, but really, I was only asking about the dress. I was looking for it tonight."

The muscles in his face tense. "Ah, she took it with her."

"Huh?"

Dad looks down at the table. "I buried her in that dress. It was her favorite. Bianca's dream was to be a clothing designer. She wanted to design clothes for mothers and daughters. Had she lived..." He breathes deep. "I know she would've been very successful."

That's when we both totally lose it. Dad throws his arms around me and I cling to him, tight. I know she would've been successful, too, if only she had been given the chance. If only the doctors had detected the tiny hole in her heart before it was too late.

pumping red

Graham calls me right when he gets back from his mini getaway, *yahoo!* He says he thought about me a lot, *double yahoo!* I tell him about *Lady in Red*, how I've chosen to hang it in the family room for all to see, rather than hogging the whole thing up in my bedroom. I even tell him about my dinner with Helga, but I leave out a thing or two. We talk late into the night, after most of the hardcore clubbers in my building have stumbled home, me snuggled under my comforter.

"Called my guidance counselor today. She let me add ceramics to my schedule." I swing my stuffed elephant around by the trunk.

"That's great. I could use a new mug." Graham laughs.

I look up at my ceiling. There are still a few glow-in-the-dark stars left from when I was going through my astronomy stage in middle school. "Don't laugh, you might get what you wish for."

"Yeah, then I can say I knew you when."

"Before *you* get famous is more like it. Your artwork is really amazing." I lick my lips and savor the heavenly taste of his kiss again.

"Thanks. It's so cool that your dad's letting me hang a couple of pieces at the gallery for the fall show." I can feel the excitement in Graham's voice. It's cute.

"I'm just happy you're going to cover the spot where *Lady in Red* was."

"Tough act to follow."

"Yes, she is." I sit up and look in the mirror on my dresser. My roots jump out at me. School starts in a few weeks. I have to decide soon if I want to go back as Licorice Chick or let the whole thing grow out.

"And I know something you're going to try on Saturday," Graham says.

"You do?"

"Yeah, I'm taking you surfing at my favorite spot down by Third Street."

"Cool, I'm up for making a fool of myself." I laugh.

"I'll bring my video camera for that." Graham laughs too.

I hear Dad's keys rustle in the front door. He's back from an art benefit. He calls my name from the kitchen. "My dad's home. I better go." I get up from my bed.

"Good night," Graham says with a yawn.

It is.

———

Liz and I meet at the beach early, before it gets overrun by tourists. Something we usually don't do. By two o'clock we're both fried and ready to go home. Coach did say to take it easy before tomorrow's game, but she didn't say deep-fry yourself.

On my way home from the beach, I pass a florist and something pulls me inside. I know Mom loved flowers and every time Dad visits her grave, he brings a bouquet, but I have never bought one for her.

I open the glass door and the bell chimes. Immediately at least twenty different scents call out to me. I'm looking for something pure, something white, just like her name. Bianca.

A tall guy with a kelly-green apron is pulling new arrivals out of a bucket. "Can I help you?"

I inch closer to the middle of the room where the smell of fresh flowers is most intense. I breathe in deep. "It's my mother's birthday tomorrow."

He's probably heard people say that a million times, but this is the first time I ever remember saying it.

"Does she have a favorite?" The man gets up from his perch. His face is partially masked by a thick beard, but I know by the sound of his voice and the way he struts that he's still pretty young.

The truth is, I don't know. I only know she liked flowers. I point to the top shelf of the refrigerator. "These are pretty."

"Gardenias. Great choice." He grabs a bunch and walks over to the cellophane-wrapping station on the counter.

"Can you use the clear wrap?" In case she's watching, I want her to be able to see them easily through the wrapping.

I hold the flowers up to my nose and sneak whiffs all the way home. I hope I haven't extracted all the smell before they get to Mom tomorrow. As usual, I'm dripping with sweat once I get inside. I place the gardenias in a vase with some water, then grab some orange juice from the fridge.

There's a package sitting on the counter. It has a little yellow sticky on it with my name. It definitely looks like a painting. I can't believe Dad already finished the one of me and Mom on the balcony. I thought it would take him months to feel ready.

It's wrapped very carefully and I have to use a knife to get off some of the masking tape. I unravel the layers of brown paper and pull out a canvas. It's not me and Mom. Just me. I was not expecting this.

I hold it up to the light. It doesn't look like Dad's usual style. It has an Andy Warhol–like quality to it. The painting is vivid and really pops out at you. It's clearly me, though. The long nose, dark hair, round eyes like Dad's. I look older, more sophisticated than I do in the end-of-the-school-year portrait. It's true I've aged this summer, and I'm not talking about all the time I've spent in the sun.

Maybe I do look a bit like Mom. Bianca Bernard, Lady in Red.

I'm wearing a light-pink tank top in the painting, and on the outside of my shirt is a red heart. The heart is 3D, mixed media. It looks like hard plastic on top of glittery sponge. I run my fingers over it. It's so shiny that it seems like the paint is still wet. My heart. How sweet.

I turn the painting over to check for an inscription, an explanation. The black print is tiny and neat. Not like Dad's usual scrawl. *Pure Red.* Then, underneath, *Graham Hadley.*

Oh my God! No he didn't? I nearly drop the painting onto the floor. I grip the sides tight and flip it back to the front. This time I notice the silhouette of a guy's face in the background. It's him. Graham, in black and white. And me in color. I stare closely at my heart. There's no hole. It's pumping red. The color of courage. The color of passion. The color of victory.

The End